THE WANDERING COWBOY

(A Novella)

RODNEY BRUCE SORKIN

Introducing Clint Walker, the Wandering Cowboy

PAGE PUBLISHING, INC.
New York, NY

First originally published by Page Publishing, Inc. 2016

ISBN 978-1-68348-576-6 (Paperback)
ISBN 978-1-68348-577-3 (Digital)

Printed in the United States of America

DEDICATION

Dedicated to my mother
Rachel Ethel Watwood Sorkin
September 23, 1903-March 7, 1950
Who loved me to excess
And left me too soon

The author wishes to express his appreciation to Larry Slavin for his assistance in editing the manuscript

As Clint Walker packed for his travel to the Virginia Military Institute, he reflected on his life growing up on a Kentucky horse farm near the town of Shelbyville. He never knew his mother as she died in childbirth. His father served as both mother and father. He taught Clint all the essentials that he would need to survive in an often-dangerous world.

Firearms training began when Clint was ten years old—rifle, shotgun, and handgun. Clint practiced several hours each day for aim, accuracy, and speed. He became very proficient in the skill. Once, they were looking for deer in a wooded area nearby, when they spooked a deer who took off like lightning. Although mostly hidden by the trees, Clint snapped a shot that was deadly accurate, and the deer dropped. While dressing the deer, they were surprised by a black bear, which raised itself on its hind legs, snarled, and went for the two hunters. Clint's father had left his firearm leaning against a tree a good ten feet away. Clint had not yet reloaded, so he swung at the bear with the stock of his rifle, hitting it by the side of its head. The bear was not at all deterred from its objective but was momentarily distracted. In that second or two, Clint reloaded his rifle and shot the bear through its upper palate and brain, dropping it down dead. From this experience, Clint learned to always reload his firearm at the first opportunity. They would often go hunting like this and Clint always bagged more than his fair share of the haul.

Clint was also taught to respect wildlife and never kill unless you needed the animal for food or its hide for clothes or shelter.

The community of landholders around Shelbyville held fairs and neighborly gatherings throughout the year. At one of these affairs, Clint got first prize in a shooting contest. He was twelve; all of the others were twenty and older.

Clint became obsessed with the quick draw. He practiced day and night, until he was so fast that his pistol seemed to appear in his hand by magic. His father told him that "being fast was not good enough. One had to be both fast and accurate." As a result, Clint practiced with bottles resting on empty barrels. He would draw and shoot each of the bottle as fast as he could. They even instituted such a contest at the county fair. Clint took home the blue ribbon every time.

Next were lessons in hand combat. Clint was taught by an itinerant monk from Tibet. He learned how to punch and to kick with power while defending himself. At school one day, Clint was attacked by the school bully and two of his friends. Clint punched the leader in the nose, breaking it and putting the attacker out of the fight. The second rushed at Clint and received a kick in the solar plexus, putting him on the ground, gasping for breath. The third ran away. No one bothered Clint after that incident.

Clint could not remember when he first rode on a horse. His father told him it was about the time that he started to walk. Of course, with Clint growing up on a horse farm, he became very close to horses. On his seventeenth birthday, his father gave him a special present. A baby colt had just been born that was perfect in every way. He was black in color, except for a white diamond on his forehead, and white socks above his hooves. Clint named him Blackie and doted on him with special treats and rubdowns. Soon Blackie would follow Clint everywhere he went, except when Clint went to school. However, as soon as Clint returned, Blackie would neigh and kick the stall until Clint appeared.

Next to Blackie, Clint's best friend was Marylou McDonald. Marylou lived on a farm adjacent to Clint. As children, they played together and once got into trouble by taking a long walk to picnic by the river. "Marylou, this food is delicious!" stated Clint.

"I made it myself, and one day, I will cook for my husband just the same way."

"Clint, what do you want to be when you grow up?" asked Marylou.

"I want to be a lawman," replied Clint. "But I suppose that I will have to be a horse breeder."

Marylou's parents became wild with worry when they couldn't find her. They were joined by Clint's father, looked high and low, and finally saw them by the river walk. The two youngsters looked with dread as they were approach by Marylou's parents and Clint's father—all looking quite upset. They were both punished for their lack of consideration. As Marylou and Clint matured, their strong bond turned into love. They became inseparable. When Clint achieved an appointment to the Virginia Military Institute, Clint and Marylou promised to stay true to each other, and it was understood that they would marry when Clint returned.

— Four years later —

The steamboat dock in Cincinnati was bustling with cargo, workers, and passengers. Clint Walker looked down at the busy and noisy scene from the foredeck of the *State of Ohio* steamship. Grain, coal, whiskey, and manufactured goods were being loaded for shipment down south, with a final destination of New Orleans. Clint Walker had begun his river voyage at Parkersburg, Virginia. He proudly wore the single bar of a second lieutenant in the US Army cavalry, having completed a four-year course of study at the Virginia Military Institute. The training was vigorous and the conditions were Spartan at the institute. On this beautiful June day in the year 1860, clouds of acrimony, dissension, and anger marred the relations between the abolitionist northern states and the southern slave states.

The Ohio River passed by many states at odds over the slavery question and portrayed the divisions of this great nation. Beginning in Pennsylvania, a free state, the river flowed by Virginia (slave), Ohio (free), Kentucky (slave), Indiana (free), and Illinois (free), before joining the Mississippi river, which flowed south by the slave states of

Missouri, Tennessee, Arkansas, Mississippi, and Louisiana. The Ohio River was, in fact, the boundary between the free and slave states.

Clint couldn't wait to get to his home near Shelbyville, Kentucky. His father owned Pleasant Acres, one of the best horse farms, raising saddlebred mounts. Clint hadn't known his mother. She had died at childbirth. His father, a rough-hewn workingman, had raised Clint as both mother and father. He would be very proud of Clint upon his arrival.

Clint's thoughts returned to his time at VMI. The institute had placed honor above all things. Clint had had the benefit of studying under some of the best military men in the army—men who had seen combat in the Mexican war. Professor Thomas Jackson had taught physics and science, and had taught Clint's class on artillery. Clint had been one of the eighty-five cadets who had been sent to Charles Town under Professor Jackson to help maintain order during the execution of John Brown.

Clint had also met and become friends with Lieutenant James Stuart who had stopped by VMI on his way back to Washington from Charles Town. Stuart, who was a cavalryman through and through, had served as Aide de Camp to Col. Robert Lee during the capture of John Brown at the US Army Arsenal at Harper's Ferry. Clint had admired the dashing and stylishly dressed cavalryman.

Clint's best friend Matt Waltman and he had had many an adventure while at VMI. They had helped each other succeed. Clint finished first in his class in swordsmanship, marksmanship, and the art of military horsemanship. The last was a cinch because Clint had grown up riding horses as soon as he had taken his first steps. Matt was probably the better boxer and brawler, as they had discovered during one weekend pass in Lexington, when someone in a saloon had insulted VMI cadets. Matt, who had also received a commission in the army cavalry, would be coming up to spend a month with Clint at the ranch.

Beyond the bustle of the wharf lay the city of Cincinnati, one of the great American cities. Clint took in the view of factories, restaurants, shops, and homes. The south shipped cotton to Cincinnati, which turned it into cloth. The cloth was then returned to the south and used to make clothing. Both slave and Free State benefitted from the exchange, and it was hard to see that any benefit could come from separating the states. Abolitionism had spread in the north like a contagious sickness with a religious fervor. The abolitionists did not realize or care what damage they were doing to the nation. Eliminating slavery would have a devastating effect upon the south's economy and impoverish most southerners, or so Clint thought.

Clint's trip home would take ten days. It began in Lexington, Virginia, from where he took a stagecoach to Parkersburg. That was a three-day trip with overnight stays at Beckley and Charles Town, where he changed coaches. On the fourth day, he boarded the steamship *Queen City*, which traveled on the Ohio River between Pittsburg and Paducah, Kentucky. The voyage took another five days, with ten stops between Petersburg and Louisville, his destination. Clint had been lucky to book a stateroom. Most passengers slept on deck amidst cordage and freight, or in one of the common cabins like the bar or dining room. After arriving in Louisville in the evening, Clint would book a hotel room for the night and then catch the morning train to Shelbyville, which arrived at noon. It was there the next morning that his father would meet him with a carriage for the ride home.

Clint proceeded to the Crown Hotel after arriving in Shelbyville. The town had changed little since Clint had left for college. The steeple of the First Baptist Church still towered over all the other buildings in town. The Crown Hotel was a three-story structure with reception, tavern, reading room, and dining room on the first floor. Four outhouses stood in the back of the hotel for use by guests, diners, and visitors. Clint knew Homer, the desk clerk, who cheerfully greeted him and gave him a key to a corner room on the second floor. Clint was awakened by a chambermaid at sunup who brought him a fresh pot of coffee. After washing, shaving, and getting dressed in his army uniform, Clint went downstairs to await the arrival of his father. He found an outside chair on the wooden walkway in front of the hotel.

Within a half-hour, Clint saw a carriage approach the hotel. Driving the carriage was Henry, the family house servant, instead of his father. The carriage had no sooner stopped than Henry jumped down and approached Clint with hat in hand and tears in his eyes. "Masser Clint, I's got bad news for you. Yo daddy don had a heart attack and passed last night." Henry, who had been his friend and companion since early childhood, embraced Clint and they both cried. Clint felt a great emptiness; he was now alone in the world.

Somehow Clint managed to work his way through the next couple of weeks as his father was given a Christian burial and the estate was settled. One day he called Henry into the library. "Henry, you have faithfully served us for twenty years or more. In view of that service, I am setting you free. Now you have a choice. You can stay here. If you do, you will receive a workman's wage, and we will build you a cabin to live in and you will have a plot of land to grow vegetables and keep chickens. If you marry one of our people, I will set her free too, and your children will be born free. If you decide to leave, I will give you papers proving that you are a freedman, and you will get a horse with tackle, and some money to cover your initial expenses before you find work."

"Massa Clint, I don know what to say, 'cept I thank you with all my heart. I stay here to take care o you."

Clint had left part of his heart behind when he left for VMI. That part of his heart belonged to Marylou McDonald. They had pledged themselves to each other before Clint left for VMI, and Marylou had promised to wait for Clint. During the funeral, Marylou had been the strong shoulder upon which Clint had found refuge. Clint now rode over to the McDonald's spread, and knocked at the open front door. "Come on in, Clint," said John McDonald. "Let me once again extend my utmost condolences to you upon the loss of your father."

"Thank you, Mr. McDonald," replied Clint.

"Sir, I am the sole heir of my father's estate, and I now own the family ranch. I tell you this so that you will know that I can provide for a wife. I have long been in love with Marylou, and I believe that feeling is mutual. Well then, sir, I am seeking your permission to ask your daughter for her hand in marriage!"

Mr. McDonald smiled with amusement at the young man's fluster, and responded, "Clint, I felt that you might get around to asking me for Marylou someday. I have watched you two lovebirds over the years. If Marylou will have you, you will have my blessing." Clint wasted no time in finding Marylou. She was out by the corral with her horse, anticipating a ride with Clint. Clint mounted his horse and stepped over to the corral. "Marylou, how about going for a ride?"

"Swell," she answered. She mounted her Cleveland Bay/thoroughbred mix horse named Jumper, and they rode off toward Guist Creek Lake. Once at the creek, they dismounted and sat to watch the waterfowl on the lake. "Penny for your thoughts," said Clint. Marylou looked up at the few white fluffy clouds in the otherwise azure blue sky and answered, "I'm thinking about how great God is to create this marvelous world." Clint picked up a wild daisy and began picking petals off, one by one, saying "she loves me, she loves me not" with each petal. Unfortunately, there were an even number of petals on this particular wildflower, and Clint ended with "she loves me not." So Clint looked at Marylou with a plaintiff look and said, "Tell me that that's not true, that you don't love me anymore!"

"My darling, I love you now, and I always will!" responded Marylou.

"In that case, marry me," said Clint on bended knee and holding forth a beautiful diamond ring.

"Why, Clint, I do declare, you take my breath away, you unpredictable boy," said Marylou as her face blushed red. "Of course, I will marry you anytime you say, and I will be a good and loving wife too!"

"It's set then! I promise to always love you and care for you. You have made me the happiest man alive!" Clint gathered Marylou in his arms, and as his hand brushed her hair from her eyes, he kissed her, first gently, then urgently, and said. "Let's tell your parents and then set a date."

They set the wedding date for Saturday, September 14, the place to be the Baptist Church in Shelbyville with the reception at Marylou's parents' estate.

Throughout the year, the divisions between the states over slavery had become heated. Within Kentucky itself, opinion was evenly divided. State political leaders sought to position Kentucky as a mediator between north and south. As an important border state both sides eyed Kentucky as a potential ally, but neither side wanted Kentucky to mediate. Governor Magoffin leaned toward the south, while the legislature leaned toward the north.

Clint excitedly dressed for the last foxhunt of the season. In his scarlet jacket, white breeches, and English black boots, he looked quite resplendent upon Blackie, his favorite saddlebred. Clint had melted many young female hearts while on the hunt. He joined the others at the club. They would begin the hunt at Pritchard's pasture and woods, where red foxes were abundant. Marylou McDonald stole furtive looks at her beloved Clint as she prepared for the hunt. She wore a black velvet-trimmed jacket, with tan pants and black leather boots. She would ride in the less demanding second field while Clint was in the first field, so she would escape his attention until they had caught their prey.

The hounds were cast by the huntsman and, picking up a scent, began running and barking. The hunters raced to follow the pack. Clint urged Blackie forward as he took the lead following the pack, which were all kept together by the whips. Clint came to the first obstacle, a split-rail fence, and urged Blackie to jump over it, which he did with a foot to spare. The lucky fox found a burrow and went to ground. The hounds milled about the burrow, howling with disappointment. The huntsman led them away and they finally found another scent. Off they went, and the hunters followed. This time the pack caught up with the fox and quickly killed it. The huntsman took the brush, pads, and mask trophies and threw the remaining carcasses to the pack. The hunters then returned to the club for conversation and refreshments. Clint particularly enjoyed the hunt for the thrill of the chase, as well as for the social opportunities that followed.

"That hillbilly Lincoln is a real danger to our livelihood, I tell you!" stated Thomas Gilmore within Clint's hearing. That seemed to be the main topic on most of the horsemen's minds. Clint worked his way over to John McDonald. "Clint, you rode well today. I held my breath on the first jump, but you cleared it handedly."

"Thank you, sir. It is good of you to say so. I know you were right behind me and met every obstacle," replied Clint.

"Well, that's good of you to say, Clint, but I feel like old age is creeping up on me, and it's getting harder and harder to complete the course. Anyway, you don't want to spend time with an old man. Yonder is Marylou who is by herself."

Clint worked his way over to Marylou.

"Clint, I'm worried. Everybody is talking about our state seceding from the Union if Mr. Lincoln is elected president."

"Why, my darling Marylou, now don't you worry yourself. It's not going to happen, although you can understand why they are worried. If Lincoln is elected and frees the slaves, we will all go bankrupt and our way of life will be destroyed. However, our state has declared itself to be neutral—to serve as a peacemaker and negotiate between the northern and southern states to find a solution acceptable to both sides."

"Clint, I love the way you know these things. It brings such comfort and reassurance to me."

As September arrived, Matt Waltman, Clint's best friend from VMI, arrived for a month's visit. He would also serve as Clint's best man. As the wedding day arrived, both gentlemen looked splendid in their Army dress uniforms, armed with swords. The marriage was the biggest society news of the year. Consequently, the church was packed to capacity.

Many of the local onlookers thought that Marylou was about the prettiest bride that the town had seen in a long time. Pastor Phillips conducted the ceremony.

"Would you please face each other and join hands. Clint, do you take Marylou to be your wife? Do you promise to love, honor, cherish, and protect her, forsaking all others and holding only to her forevermore?" Clint looked dreamingly into Marylou's eyes and responded, "I do."

"Marylou, do you take Clint to be your husband? Do you promise to love, honor, cherish, and obey him, forsaking all others and holding only to him forevermore?" Marylou trembled slightly as she looked with love into Clint's eyes and responded, almost in a whisper, "I do."

"Then in the eyes of God, and by the power invested in me by the Commonwealth of Kentucky, I pronounce you man and wife! Clint, you may kiss the bride. What therefore God hath joined together, let not man put asunder."

Then began a period that Clint would remember as a happy time. Marylou joined him at Pleasant Acres and Clint concentrated on running the saddlebred horse business. Clint acquired a fine thoroughbred for stud that he used to improve the herd.

In November Abraham Lincoln was elected president at the head of a new political party, the Republican Party. Before President Lincoln assumed his office, South Carolina, in December of 1860, seceded from the union. Within two months, Mississippi, Florida, Alabama, Georgia, Louisiana and Texas followed suit. On February 9, the Confederate States of America was formed by the seceding states and Jefferson Davis was elected president. Kentucky wanted no part of secession and did not want to take sides. On the contrary, it wanted to mediate between them. On March 4, 1861, Abraham Lincoln was sworn in as the sixteenth president of the United States. In his inaugural address, he took great pains to assure the southern states that he would not interfere with their "peculiar" system of Negro slavery.

In spite of such assurances, hotheaded southerners under General Beauregard fired on Fort Sumter in Charleston harbor on April 12, 1861. On April 15, President Lincoln telegraphed Gov. Magoffen asking for seventy-five thousand troops to help put down the incipient rebellion. As these events unfolded, Clint watched with increasing unease the threat to his homeland and his ranch. The army concentrated troops in Indiana, opposite Louisville at Camp Joe Holt. That was only thirty-five miles from Shelbyville. More troops were poised to invade Kentucky from Camp Clay in Newport, Ohio, ninety miles away.

In early April, Matt returned for a visit. He was excited about a meeting he had had with JEB. Stuart in Lexington, Virginia. Virginia was forming an army to protect its sovereignty, and Stuart was expecting to be given a cavalry command in a brigade under Col. Thomas Jackson, to be formed to protect the Shenandoah Valley. Matt had been offered a commission in the Virginia army cavalry once the unit was formed.

Clint had been mulling things over in his mind. The US Army troop concentrations on Kentucky's northern border were meant to threaten and intimidate. The one across the river from Louisville was only a day's ride away. If the North invaded Kentucky, they would bring the horrors of war to a neutral law-abiding state. Clint could not be a part of that. Nevertheless, Clint could not see himself taking up arms against his own country.

Almost one hour after Matt arrived, a courier came riding up with a telegram addressed to Lieutenant Clint Walker. The telegram stated, "You are hereby ordered to report to Camp Joe Holt, Indiana, for duty in the US Army cavalry, no later than 1900 hours on 30 April 1861." The decision point had arrived. Clint would not fight against his fellow Kentuckians who would resist invasion by Union troops, or his fellow VMI Virginians for that matter. He asked the courier to wait a minute, and found Matt in the house. "Matt, do you think Jeb Stuart would give me a commission in his cavalry? If so, I will join you."

"Clint, I don't think that would be a problem at all," answered Matt.

After assuring himself that the ranch and Marylou would be well cared for by consulting with the ranch manager and Henry, Clint wrote out his resignation from the US Army, and sent it back with the courier. He then gathered his essential travel kit and weapons, saddled Blackie, spent a tearful quarter hour with Marylou, and left with Matt on the road to Virginia.

CHAPTER 2

Clint remembered his first day as a Confederate officer. It was May 12. He and Matt traveled to Harper's Ferry, on the Potomac River, where Col. Thomas Jackson had been stationed to guard the central approach to Virginia through the Shenandoah Valley. There Lt. Col. Stuart commanded the First Virginia Cavalry Regiment of the Army of the Shenandoah. It was a regiment in name only, having only twenty-one officers and three hundred thirteen troopers. Stuart temporarily organized the regiment into two companies, Able and Baker companies, each with 155 troopers. Since Clint and Matt had both graduated from a military academy, Stuart chose them to lead the two companies. The remaining officers and men formed a headquarters company.

Clint was put to work traveling between Army outposts guarding the Potomac crossings. On a sunny day in early July, he rejoiced over the fields filled with wildflowers of contrasting colors, yellow buttercups and dandelions, blue violets, white chickweed, and pink columbines,. A cloud of dust signaled a cavalry patrol headed toward Clint's company. Spurring his mount into action, Clint led his troopers forward toward the unwanted invaders. Seeing the approaching Confederate force, the invaders let loose a volley of carbine shots and retreated back across the river. One of the bullets tore a hole through Clint's shirt, while leaving a bleeding path through the skin of his left rib cage. That was the only time Clint was wounded during the war.

The Confederate Cavalry grew quickly during this period of the war. A brigade was formed and Col. Stuart was promoted to lead it. His place as commander of the regiment was taken by Col. Turner Ashby.

Clint was promoted twice, initially to First Lieutenant, and then to Captain. Matt was promoted to First Lieutenant. Alpha Company expanded to two hundred troops with Clint as Commander, and Matt was assigned to be Deputy Company Commander. Clint's superior rank and position over Matt did not harm their close relationship; in fact, Matt welcomed the opportunity to work at Clint's side.

The saloon in Manassas Junction was filled with the usual Saturday night crowd. Clint sat at a corner table with his back to the wall enjoying some Kentucky Bourbon when he heard raised voices at an adjacent table where poker was being played. The conflict was between two troopers and was quite heated. Clint said, "That's enough, men." The soldier next to Clint swung his arm around, pushing Clint back, and said, "Stay out of this captain. This bastard's a cheater!"

Clint grabbed the trooper under his left shoulder and shoved him down on to the table as his revolver instantaneously appeared in his right hand. "Stand down!" said Clint. The players looked amazed as they took their seats. Clint added, "Don't forget, men, the enemy's up north. Save your energy for them." He then holstered his revolver and walked out of the saloon. The placed buzzed with talk about him after he left.

Clint walked to his tent and met Matt there. "I didn't think I would have to play sheriff," said Clint as he shook his head in dismay. Matt responded, "They're on edge now, Clint. The big invasion by the bluecoats is going to happen any day now."

Clint, with Able Company, was assigned to watch the Potomac River crossings north of Harper's Ferry for a distance of twenty-five miles. Clint led his company north to the end of his watch line, and then headed back dropping off squads of six troopers every mile with instructions to report any activity immediately to Harper's Ferry. At dusk, Clint saw a squad ride in. "Sir, the Yankees are assembling a large force in Williamsport." By dusk, Clint had gathered in his company and set watching the union troops crossing the Potomac. He estimated the force as division strength. They were heading toward Martinsburg. General Joseph Johnson, when informed of the crossing, ordered Col. Jackson to resist the advance if possible, but retreat if pressed with great strength.

An orderly came up to Clint, saluted, and said, "Colonel Ashby wants you to be ready to move out first thing in the morning. All company commanders are asked to attend a meeting with him at twenty hundred hours." Clint and Matt got busy alerting their platoons to the move and organizing the mobile artillery for deployment. At 2000 hours Clint reported to Col. Ashby's headquarters, as ordered. Col. Ashby addressed the assembled commanders, "A Union force, estimated to be of division strength has crossed the Potomac near Williamsport and is moving on Martinsburg. General Stuart is ordered to delay the Union advance with our brigade. We will move out at first light tomorrow.

Union General Robert Patterson brought up his entire division to the Williamsport crossing. At Hainesville, Jackson deployed his brigade behind Hoke's run. Clint's company was held in reserve to protect Jackson's left flank. Clint watched the mountain pass with field glasses as he heard the thunder of battle before him. He saw a company-sized group of Union soldiers debouch from the pass and line up in attack position. Urging his men forward, Clint led a charge at the intruders. Seeing the cavalry charge was enough for the bluecoats. They retreated after being forced back by overwhelming Confederate pressure. Jackson's stance had also sufficiently delayed the Union force to enable Confederate General Joseph Johnson to deploy his Army of nine regiments in defense of Manassas Junction. Confederate General P. G. T. Beauregard, with the army of Northern Virginia took positions at Bull Run. The Union Army attacked with a strong feint across Bull Run, and attempted a strong attack on the Confederate left.

Clint observed telltale signs of the enemy wavering at the point of retreat, and knew this was the time to collapse their line. "Able Company, prepare to charge. Come on lads, Now Charge!" Clint's company of troopers surged forward, screaming the rebel yell, firing their pistols as they galloped toward the Union Army troops deployed along the Manassas-Sudley Road. First one, then another, and then all, of the enemy line ran away from the charging cavalry, abandoning their cannons. Clint, sword in hand, chased after the retreating union troops, slashing one after another, until they turned and raised their arms in surrender. Clint, along with the rest of Stuart's command, continued to chase the fleeing Yankees. On they went, accumulating more prisoners along the way. Finally, after a dozen miles, they decided they had gone far enough, Sending prisoners back under guard had so depleted their ranks that they were now a dozen men chasing a thousand.

Stuart had held the left flank of the Confederate Army, against the determined attempt of the Union to circle around the defenders. On Stuart's right, Jackson had held the Confederate line on Henry Hill against a Union force ten times more numerous. His determined stance with a regiment of 380 men and one cannon against a fully equipped Union Brigade would earn Thomas Jackson the sobriquet "Stonewall Jackson" ever since.

The victory for the Confederate Army was complete. The Union force disintegrated into a fleeing mob, running into the safety of Washington, and discarding their arms along the way. The civilian spectators who chose to picnic on grounds overlooking the battle also hurried back to Washington.

Summer turned into fall and fall into winter and then winter into spring. During this time, General George McClellan built up, organized, and trained the Union army. The major portion of the Confederate army secretly withdrew to Culpepper, leaving phony cannons called Quaker guns overlooking Washington to hold the Union army in place, menacing Washington by this deception.

Stonewall Jackson was promoted to a major general commanding all Confederate cavalry, and Jeb Stuart to brigadier general.

CHAPTER 3

Clint sat on a tree stump writing a letter to Marylou. Since Kentucky had joined the union side, it would take some doing to get the letter to her. The western counties of Virginia had treacherously seceded from Virginia and formed a new state on the Union side, so he could mail it in West Virginia as the opportunity arose.

> Dearest Marylou,
>
> I miss you more than words can express. Every night I yearn to be with you as I imagine what you are doing. I see you plainly in my mind. Are you well my darling? Are the Yankees bothering you at all?
>
> The fight goes well for us. I have not been in any sort of danger, for I want to return to you in one piece.
>
> The B&O Railroad passes through territory that we control, so if you send mail to me general delivery at the Martinsburg post office, I can pick it up. That is where I will mail this letter. My wonderful wife I will close now for I must get some sleep. I embrace you with my whole being, for I love you with my whole heart.
>
> Your Clint

An orderly arrived, summoning Clint to Col. Ashby's tent. Col. Ashby had a large tent, as befitted a brigade commander, with a map table and several chairs. "Gentlemen, General Jackson has ordered the fifth infantry to destroy the B & O railroad bridge at Cherry Run and Col. Imboden's brigade to cut the track at Point of Rocks. This will trap a large number of locomotives at the main switchyard in Blacksburg. The Confederacy needs locomotives, and we are going to borrow some from the Yankees! We have been ordered to protect Imboden's flank. We move out in the morning at first light. Take a look at the map here to check your route. Any questions? Good. Let's get some rest."

"It was the craziest thing you ever saw," Clint wrote to his wife. "General Jackson required the trains to pass only for two hours around noon. There was so much traffic that they got bunched up in the railroad yard at Martinsburg. We then cut the line at Point of Rocks and marched into Martinsburg and took charge of all the trains there. We burned the cars that were mostly filled with coal and helped ourselves to the tools and machines in the rail yard. General Jackson said that the South needed locomotives, so we picked the best ones we could find, eight in all, and took them apart and transported them by forty mule teams to the rail line at Strasburg, where they were taken south on the Manassas Gap Railroad. Before we left the area, we burned all the B & O railroad bridges, so the Yankees couldn't use the railroad for some time. We then rode over to one of the Potomac River dams and blew it up so the water in the C & O Canal would drop and cut the use of that waterway.

"Wouldn't you know, a large force of Yankees then came out of nowhere, and is attacking us. We are going to draw back, so I got to end here and mail the letter before we leave. I guess we can't write to each other until we drive the Yankees out of Kentucky. Be well my darling wife, your Clint."

They were indeed driven out of Martinsburg. The Yankees came in division strength against their brigade. Col. Ashby was ordered to withdraw while delaying the Union force as much as possible. They formed a defense line behind the Hoke's Run near Hainesville and held the Union force there for a day, before withdrawing to Winchester. The Union force didn't follow, however, but later withdrew to Harper's Ferry.

Union forces occupied Kernstown. Having been told by residents that the Union force there was only a brigade, Jackson decided to strike and retake the town. The attack ran into a beehive of bullets and cannon shells. Regrouping, Jackson ordered Col. Ashby's cavalry to attack around the Union left flank. Clint formed his troop up behind the Confederate center, in reserve. Screaming the rebel yell, Ashby's cavalry charged forward. They were met by a murderous fire. They faltered and the surviving troops retreated, closely followed by a Union cavalry counter attack. Clint was ordered forward to protect the retreating Confederate cavalry and urged his men forward toward the attacking Union force. They were met headlong in a melee of flying bullets and clashing swords. Clint headed for the Union Commander who shot at him with his pistol but missed. He didn't get a second chance. Clint closed with him and slashed the officer's neck with his saber. The man received a fatal blow as blood spewed out of his severed Carotid artery. Clint looked around for another target and saw that the Union force faltered and fled. This time it was the Confederate cavalry that urged them on. Clint sounded the recall and the troopers returned to the Confederate line.

March gave way to April as winter turned into spring. Robins appeared along with finches; and azaleas, snowdrops, and forsythias burst into bloom. Clint rested when he could with thoughts of his darling wife Marylou. "Was she okay? Would he ever see her again? Did she miss him as much as he missed her? Damn this war!"

During the transition period, there were constant skirmishes with the Union troops, who constantly probed the Confederate positions.

Alarming news now arrived that the Yankees had landed a large army, fully equipped, on Fort Monroe—a still held Union fortress at the southern tip of the Virginia peninsula. The Yankees had only to march up the peninsula to take Richmond. There was little to stop them. Most of the Confederate Army of Virginia, until recently in Northern Virginia, had withdrawn to Culpeper, about ninety miles from Richmond. Defending Richmond on the peninsula was only Gen. John Magruder's eleven thousand men, outnumbered probably by ten to one. There were nine thousand troops in Norfolk under Gen. Huber. General Stuart was ordered to rush his cavalry down to Richmond to augment the forces there until Gen. Johnson could arrive with the Army of Virginia. After several days travel Clint caught up with General Johnson's main force and took position as a rear guard. Clint had them take cover on either side of the Williamsburg road, armed with their carbines. Not more than one-half hour later a cloud of dust announced the arrival of the trailing Union force. A cavalry unit, riding four abreast, was in the vanguard. They didn't see the trap until it was too late. Shots rang out from the Confederate line and the first few rows were decimated. The troopers behind began circling around to flank Clint, who ordered his trooper to fall back at a gallop. Clint's duty was to delay the Yankees, not to fight them. They found a spot where the road became sunken and turned to the right—a natural ambush location. Off the road was a meadow of green grass and wild flowers. It began to rain. The meadow filled with waves of wind-blown rain. After ten minutes, the rain ceased and the sun broke through the clouds, bringing a promise of newness and warmth. Streaks of red and orange crossed the blue and white sky. The meadowlarks sang with joy and were joined by chickadees, cardinals, and blue jays. Once again the trailing Union cavalry came down the road toward the well positioned Confederates. A stinging hail of bullets cut through the ranks of the Yankees.

Clint again retreated, this time to the line of redoubts defending the Williamsburg to Yorktown road, where the Confederate Army was prepared to make a stand. Clint was ordered to take his company to redoubt number 6 in the center of the line. It was an earthen fortification with fifteen-foot high walls nine feet thick and protected by a dry moat nine feet deep. His men were deployed along the south facing edge of the elongated pentagon-shaped fortification between two cannon. They were immediately assaulted by the Union main body. A maelstrom of leaded shot and exploding cannon shells fell on the defenders. Hordes of men in blue uniforms assailed the fortification, standing before the moat and shooting up at the Confederates. Men brought forth scaling ladders and bridged the moat by resting them on the wall. This came not without cost to the attackers. Scores of Yankees fell from the Confederate fire.

As their men fell, their places were taken by new echelons thrown into the battle. The day wore on and the sun descended into the west. Finally the exhausted Union force had no more to give to the blood soaked ground and pulled back. An officer carrying a white flag approached and asked for a truce to recover the dead and wounded. The request was granted. The bodies were recovered and night fell shortly after.

Clint took stock of the situation: a fifth of his troopers were dead or wounded. Any wound to the torso was invariably fatal—if not immediately, then after becoming infected. The treatment for non-superficial wounds to the limbs was usually amputation. The screams of the wounded losing limbs filled the fortification with fearful dread.

An eighth moon rose in the sky, lending some dim illumination to the men below. General Johnson decided to pull out and to move to another defense line closer to Richmond. On the outskirts of Richmond, at Fair Oaks Station, General Johnson determined that the Union Army had taken a position straddling the Chickahominy River—three corps north of the river and two corps isolated south of the river. Knowing that Richmond could not survive a siege, he decided to attack the two isolated corps where he would have a manpower advantage.

Clint and his men bivouacked at the Seven Pines crossing. The skies poured down rain in buckets as lightning forked down and thunder resounded in great loud claps. The rivers became swollen and overflowed their banks and the dirt roads became nearly impassable with mud. The troopers hunkered down in their tents, trying to stay dry while sleeping on oilcloth, lying on wet ground. Little streams formed and worked their ways to the already swollen creeks. The nature of the terrain and the heavy rain made cavalry use difficult, so the troopers would fight as infantry. General Stuart was joined with General Huber's command and the troopers, armed with rifles and positioned in the center of the line, marched through the muddy road to the south bank of the Chickahominy River. Clint formed his men up in a line and ordered, "Fix bayonets." The Union pickets, miserable in the rain, failed to immediately notice the Confederate force as it double-timed on the attack. Then all hell broke loose. The Confederates, catching the Yankees in bivouac, cut through the startled bluecoats like a hot knife through butter, shooting and bayoneting all those who did not run. The troopers ran after those trying to escape and cut many more down. The camp was theirs. Elsewhere, on either side of the troopers, the infantry crushed the Union force. Within fifteen minutes the Union reformed and rallied, charging ahead anew in ranks. Each side exchanged fire and casualties on both sides mounted. The Union line wavered, and the troops retreated in order. Clint rushed forward with his men until only fifty yards separated them from the enemy, firing round after round until the Yankees turned tail and ran.

General Johnson was wounded in this, the hardest fought and greatest casualty battle of the war, and General Lee took his place. The Union force reorganized and once more went on the attack—this time at Oak Grove, where, if successful, Richmond would be under the siege guns of the Union army. The Yankees, with two divisions, advanced through White Oak Swamp and a terrific battle ensued. Clint, whose company was held in reserve, heard the cacophonous din of guns firing. Hours later it was over and the infantry returned, black with smoke, and marched to their barracks.

It was now June 25. General Lee began a series of six major battles in seven days that would be known in history as the Seven Days Battles. General Stuart's cavalry, assigned to probe the Union right flank for weakness found indeed that it was vulnerable, and in fact, performed a circumnavigation of the Union forces, returning with 165 prisoners, hundreds of horses and mules and a variety of captured Union supplies. General Jackson arrived after preventing Union General Banks' Army from attacking Richmond from the North, and in fact, chasing them back across the Potomac. This campaign, known as the Valley Campaign, made Jackson one of the most revered Generals of the Confederacy.

Clint, riding with Stuart, was happy to be in the saddle again with his company. They split off from the main column to reconnoiter James City. Clint divided the company into two parts, with Matt leading the second half. They entered the town on either side of Main Street, slowly working their way down to the city center. When they had reached State Street, Clint cautiously worked his way to Main Street, and spotted a platoon sized Union force assembled in the city center in front of a dry goods store and tavern. Clint hand signaled to Matt, and both troops moved on the center. The show of force was overwhelming. The Yankees had no choice but to surrender. Along with forty men, they captured two wagons, each with two mules. The supplies in the wagons were returned to the dry goods store, from where they had been requisitioned.

A young woman wearing a blue bonnet and dress stepped out on to the street and approached Clint. "Thank God you arrived, sir. Those Yankees would have threatened the women of the town and taken anything of value."

"Why, ma'am, we are happy to be of service."

"I can see that you are quite a gentleman. Please let me fix you a meal—it is the least that I can do."

"That is most kind of you, ma'am, but duty calls and I must be off with my men."

Clint understood that the woman, starved for masculine affection, wanted a Confederate soldier to share her bed. "Perhaps another time," thought Clint.

Matt had already formed the prisoners into a five man wide column behind the captured wagons. When Clint rejoined the formation they headed off, double time, to their rendezvous with Stuart at Carter's Grove.

General Lee's aggressive attacks forced McClellan to retreat to the southern tip of the peninsula. It was at this time that General Lee decided to take a gamble that turned into a brilliant strategy. Believing that the defeated Union peninsula force would no longer attempt to attack toward Richmond, Lee decided to fight the Union force descending from northern Virginia under General John Pope. This he did successfully, although outnumbered by the Union force, and defeated the Yankees a second time at Manassas.

And so it continued battle after battle, in Virginia and in Maryland, until the bloodbath near Sharpsburg, Maryland. Clint and his men fought as dismounted cavalry in the sunken road—time and again repulsing Union attacks. When it was all over it was a stalemate, but Lee pulled back from Maryland into Virginia, so the Union claimed victory. As a consequence, the European countries that had once considered joining with the Confederacy held back, and Lincoln issued the Emancipation Proclamation. For Clint the war continued. When General Lee once again invaded the north, General Stuart supported that effort by circumnavigating the Union Army, destroying Union supplies, capturing many Yankees, and bringing captured supplies to the Confederate Army at a place in Pennsylvania called Gettysburg. That bloody battle was lost, and with it the war and the Confederate Army was in full retreat. Stuart's cavalry served as rear guard, giving time for General Lee to cross the Potomac with all of his guns, supplies, and wounded. Clint had little trouble, as the Union Army did not press to cut off the retreating Confederates. There were some minor clashes with roving Union cavalry patrols, but that was all.

CHAPTER 4

The loss of Vicksburg on the Mississippi in the western theater and Lee's defeat at Gettysburg doomed the southern cause if for no other reason than to bring General Grant to President Lincoln's attention. "That man's a fighter," Lincoln is purported to have said.

"But he is a drunkard," his advisors told him.

"I don't care—he fights. Find out what he drinks and send a barrel to every general in our army," replied Lincoln.

Unhappy with General George Meade's lack of aggressiveness in chasing the Confederate Army after Gettysburg, President Lincoln appointed General Grant to command the Union Army. Grant was like a bulldog—he'd grab hold of your haunch and wouldn't let go.

The South was in retreat, desperately trying to save Richmond. They fought in the battle of the wilderness—a bloody but inconclusive fight in the Confederate's favor by casualty count. Grant hung on and moved southeast to attempt to turn Lee's right flank, resulting in a battle at Spotsylvania. It was another bloody fight involving Clint and his men, fighting dismounted in prepared works, but in the end, nobody won except the grim reaper.

On a sunny day in May, the eleventh, while the battle continued to rage at Spotsylvania, reports arrived of a large force of Union cavalry heading into Richmond. Stuart immediately assembled his two brigades of cavalry to oppose this invasion. He interposed his cavalry between the Union force and Richmond, lining up a dismounted brigade in the shelter of a ridgeline by an old abandoned yellow tavern. General Stuart didn't know it at the time, but he was outmanned by General Sheridan's twelve thousand Union troopers to his five thousand troopers. He was also outgunned: the Union cavalry was equipped with the rapid firing Spencer carbines, whereas the Confederate cavalry had single shot Springfield carbines. The Union force attacked on foot directly at the ridgeline. The battle raged back and forth for a good three hours. Sensing a tipping point, the Union force mounted a cavalry charge that broke through the ridgeline. Clint and his men had been held in reserve along with the rest of the First Virginia brigade. Stuart knew that he had to beat back the Union cavalry or lose the day. With his sword held high and then pointing at the foe, Stuart yelled, "Forward charge!" A thousand horses charged ahead as one at the Union cavalry. Clint and his company were in the front rank along with Stuart. Targets were plentiful and bullets flew by and into them, men falling all around Clint. When they sent the Yankees in retreat and reached the ridgeline, some of the Confederate cavalry, satisfied with the outcome, pulled up at the ridgeline. Stuart, already past the ridgeline, and wanting to continue the rout, turned around to urge his men forward. Just then a Yankee who had lost his mount, pulled out his pistol, and from a distance of only thirty paces, shot Stuart in the back. The coward found his horse, mounted, and started to run back to the Union line. Clint, furious at what he had seen, urged Blackie forward and chased after the villainous trooper. At a full gallop, Clint slowly closed the gap. He drew his saber, and with one swift and mighty blow, lopped off the head of the trooper. The horse continued running until the decapitated Yankee fell off. Clint spotted a Spencer carbine in the horse's saddle holster. He took the carbine and the holster, and searched in the saddle bags for ammunition. There were hundreds of rounds, so he took those too. By this time the Union cavalry was returning, and as they got within carbine range, Clint retreated back to his unit. The battle ended, more or less, in a stand-off. After the fight, Clint got a twenty-four-hour pass. He visited a lady in Richmond that he had gotten to know and left the Spencer in her root cellar.

Clint knew that the war was lost. In early April the Union force besieging Richmond and Petersburg overwhelmed the Confederate defense and Lee began a retreat South in an attempt to join forces with General Johnson. The Union Army cut the rail line, preventing its use as an escape route. Three corps of the Confederate Army, now on foot, were closely pursued by the Union Army, which caught up with them at the crossing of Sailor's Creek. Three separate battles raged by the creek. Clint and his men fought desperately, but to no avail. Casualties mounted and rivulets of blood flowed into the creek, coloring it pink in some spots.

Some escaped by fording the creek, but the majority was forced to surrender. Clint along with 7,700 other Confederate soldiers was taken prisoner. In three days, the war was over. General Lee surrendered to General Grant at Appomattox Court House. The prisoners were lined up in ceremonial fashion in honor of the occasion. Before them stood hundreds of stacks of rifles, representing a small portion of the thousands of rifles that had been surrendered.

Under the generous terms offered by General Grant, the Confederate prisoners would be set free, soldiers who had joined the army with their own horses were permitted to leave with them, and officers were permitted to keep their side arms. Clint left with Blackie and rode into the burned out city of Richmond. He found the remnants of the house of his friend where he had stored the captured Spencer carbine. The root cellar was still intact and Clint quickly found his weapon, saddle holster, and ammunition. There were no supplies to be had so Clint headed out of town to return home empty handed.

CHAPTER 5

Clint couldn't wait to get home to his beloved Marylou, to Kentucky, and to his horse farm. It was quite a distance—about six hundred miles and required crossing the Blue Ridge Mountains. *At least a month,* thought Clint. Luckily, it was spring and the snow line would be quite high in the mountains. He had a bare minimum of food and equipment and would subsist on what game he could take.

He left on the best of terms with his brotherhood of cavalry-men. Matt and one half dozen others would look for Clint to call them up as the occasion would require. They were most anxious to continue the fellowship that had grown solid during four long years of war. They arranged for a post office box that they would check once a month.

Clint travelled to Gordonsville, and took a room at the Exchange Hotel. He had been there previously when the hotel had served as a hospital during the war. In the morning he bought a few supplies, saddled up and headed southwest to Charlottesville. After an over-night stay, he continued on the three notch road in the Shenandoah Valley through Waynesboro to Staunton. Another overnight stay in this busy bustling city, made him ready to tackle the thirty-mile trip to Lexington, home of his alma mater VMI.

Once in town Clint rode over to VMI, and renewed acquain-tances with some of the staff, arranged for a bunk for the night, and visited Stonewall Jackson's grave. Clint's feats in the war were well known throughout the school community and Clint was treated as a hero. He was given the honor of inspecting the troops on the parade grounds.

The next morning, well rested and fed, Clint headed northwest to ford the Maury River. The mountains shown in all their glory, with their beautiful blue haze that gave this part of the Appalachian Mountains their name. Clint headed south until he found the Jarmans Gap through the mountains. He worked his way by otter creek that sported hundreds of rainbow trout. The forest was filled with oak and poplar stands that gave off a fresh "woodsy" scent. Here and there wildlife appeared: elk, white tail deer, grouse, wild turkeys, wolves, raccoons, and foxes. He shot a small doe that came to the creek to drink. Clint quickly dressed the deer, taking the haunches and prime cuts. He then built a big fire and roasted all of the deer meat. Clint didn't want to meet a black bear, but he did. Clint slowly gathered his rifle, picked up a haunch, and tossed it to the bear. It was immediately taken up by the bear who started to rip it apart and take big bites. Clint then took the remaining haunches and walked to the wood line, dropping the haunches off as he went, and the last at the wood line. The bear followed the trail of the haunches and reentered the woods. Clint marveled at how Blackie had stayed rooted as he watched the spectacle.

The path afforded by the creek wound its way through the mountains without ascending to the heights. Clint made camp by the creek as dusk arrived. In a short time he had a fire going and made chicory coffee, heated some venison, and made sour dough pancakes. Using some tree limbs he made a shelter and covered it with leaf covered tree branches. He went to sleep with his carbine at his side. It rained during the night, but Clint was mostly dry thanks to the shelter. Blackie had found some grass to satisfy his hunger. Clint did not tie him down, for he would always stay with his master.

After scaling the initial set of mountains, the land opened up into a very pleasant plateau. The trail became a dirt road that passed by a number of farms. Clint saw farmers plowing their fields for the spring crop. Somewhere in the mountains, Clint had passed over into the new state of West Virginia. There were more mountains to pass, more roads to travel, but eventually Clint arrived at the Kentucky border. Two more days of travel and he entered his home horse farm, Pleasant Acres. He didn't see any horses grazing in the pasture. Clint hurried along to the house. It wasn't there! What was once his home was now the charred remains of a house. Henry's cottage was still there. Henry, the former slave that Clint had set free, who had chosen to stay on the farm and help Marylou, came out of the cottage and walked over to Clint. "Masser Clint, I's glad you come home from da war looking good. But I got bad news for you. Your misses don caught a bad sickness. I done all I could, but weren't no good and she passed, God rest her soul. And then some raiders don come and burnt your house down and took all the horses."

Clint nearly toppled over—he felt like he had charged into a brick wall. His dear wife dead and his horse farm gone! What could he do? He had nothing—nothing to count on.

Henry had stayed on and taken care of Marylou and the horse farm. He deserved to live here in peace. In the morning he would go into town and transfer the horse farm property to Henry. Henry begged him to have supper with him and his family. Clint assented. As Clint entered the cottage, he noticed how neat and livable it appeared. Henry's wife, Cora, was one of Clint's former slaves. By the agreement that Clint had formalized before he left for Virginia, she had been set free when she married Henry. They had two young children—a boy of about three years and a girl less than one year. Cora fixed a marvelous meal of stewed chicken, greens, corn, and corn bread.

Clint slept in Henry's cottage that night and, after taking care of transferring the horse farmland to Henry, headed west to Springfield Missouri. The Union had controlled Missouri during the war, but as a border state it had many southern supporters. Springfield was a bustling town that had built a manufacturing infrastructure during the war and from which it had profited, but it still had a wild west feel, having recently being the scene in the town square of the Wild Bill Hickok—Davis Tutt shootout.

Clint, having only a few dollars of US legal tender, went in search of a job. He found one at the Wells Fargo office as a driver and guard for shipment stagecoaches. His first run was to take a payroll by himself to a tanning factory in the nearby town of Bolivar and return with some passengers. Clint headed out with his six-horse stagecoach down the Highline Trail on a beautiful sunny day in the land of the Ozarks. When he slowed down to cross the Spring Creek ford, two masked men on horseback emerged from a nearby copse and, with drawn guns, shouted, "Hold up!" Clint hauled on the reins and drew to a stop.

"Throw down the money box!" yelled one of the bandits. Clint replied "sure" and—standing up to pick up the money box, which was next to him—threw it over toward the creek. The bandits looked away at the flight of the box, and Clint took that opportunity to draw his six-gun and shouted, "Drop your guns!" Both bandits turned around and leveled their guns on Clint. Clint had no choice but to blaze away at the two, who were only able to get off a wild shot or two, before dropping with several gunshot wounds. One was dead, the other wounded with a shot in his chest. Clint tore off the dead man's shirt to make bandages for the wounded man. He was able to bind the wound so the man could breathe, although Clint's experience was that these types of sucking wounds were invariably fatal.

Clint put the two in the stagecoach and, after retrieving the money box, continued on his way. Bolivar was a small town with a large tannery. Providentially, the county sheriff was in town and, taking charge of the two bodies, told Clint that the two were wanted dead or alive for armed robbery and murder, and Clint was due reward money of four hundred dollars.

Most of the tannery workers came from Springfield, and worked three weeks in Bolivar, staying in accommodations provided by the company, and returned to Springfield the fourth week. It didn't seem to make much sense to Clint—why not have the factory in Springfield? Apparently the owner lived in a mansion near Bolivar, and the area had a good source of tannins used in the process. Clint fit six very smelly workers in the stagecoach and a seventh next to him in the shotgun position, and headed home. He returned to Springfield without incident. A telegraph from the sheriff had preceded him. The reward money of four hundred Yankee dollars was waiting for him at the Wells-Fargo office, and his boss, elated at the demise of the bandits who had been stealing Wells-Fargo shipments, added an additional one hundred dollars. Clint, ready to move on, gave a month's notice. He had heard that the Kansas Pacific Railroad would be pushed west to Abilene Kansas to ship cattle to the east coast, making that small town grow, and providing opportunities.

As Clint rode into Abilene, he noticed the busy climate. Railroad workers were busy gathering supplies, construction workers were erecting buildings, and work was proceeding on a train station with track being laid. A good number of the workers were Chinese. In town, cowboys from local ranches had assembled to drive cattle at the present railhead at Springfield. Raucous sounds came from Mulroney's bar where the cowboys congregated. Clint pulled up at the Abilene hotel, across the street from the bar. Suddenly a group of three drunken cowboys spilled from the bar with one of the Chinese workers in tow and began beating him unmercifully. Clint could not look the other way. Running over to the scene, he shouted, "Stop— leave him be!"

"This ain't none of your business, mister, this here chink went into the white man's bar. Now get the hell out of here before we do it to you," replied one of the cowboys. Clint, angered, grabbed ahold of the cowboy doing the punching and threw him down to the ground. The other two went for Clint. He decked one with a haymaker to the head, and used the rushing momentum of the second to toss him over his shoulder to the ground. The first cowboy, now on his feet, started to go for his six gun, but in a lighting draw, Clint had his out and leveled at the cowboy. "Don't try it son," said Clint. The cowboy released hold of his gun. "Now boys, no harm's been done, here's a dollar, have a drink on me." The trio shook themselves off and went back into the bar. The Chinese worker, who didn't speak English, stood up and bowed to Clint, then ran back to the train station workplace.

Clint checked into the hotel, arranged for Blackie's care at the stable, ate a light supper at the hotel, and collapsed into bed.

CHAPTER 6

Clint was awakened by brisk knocking at his door. He shook the cobwebs out of his head and walked to the door. A group of men asked to come in. "Sir, we represent all of the businesses in town, as well as the God fearing citizens. My name is Myron Goodman and I own the dry goods store in town. I am also the chairman of the town council. We have no lawman to keep the peace, and having observed the way you took care of those drunken cowboys yesterday, we want to offer you the job of marshal of our fair town. We are prepared to offer you a salary commensurate with your responsibilities, say one hundred dollars per month, considering that we will soon have the railroad here and hundreds of cowboys bringing cattle and coming to town. We are also prepared to build you an office and jail, and provide living quarters. So can we count on you?"

Clint thought about it for a moment and could see no reason to turn it down; he needed a job and the pay was good, and he enjoyed law enforcement and he was good at it. "Is there a budget for deputies?"

"Yes, we have set aside funds for three deputies."

"Okay, it's a deal—I'll take the job. To whom do I report?"

"Well, you work for the council through its chairman—that would be me," replied Myron, adding, "As of now you are on the payroll. We will contract for the marshal's office and quarters before the week ends. Congratulations! Here is your badge."

Clint walked with the council members to the newspaper office where he was introduced to the editor. He then went in search of a temporary residence to stay until his quarters were completed. The widow Elsa Maxwell, recommended by Myron, took on borders and provided breakfast and dinner, and Clint decided to take a room there. The widow Elsa Maxwell turned out to be surprisingly young, shapely, and pretty, with rosy cheeks, freckles, and blonde hair that flowed down to tease her blue eyes. She welcomed Clint with a smile and showed Clint to his room cheerfully, ending by asking Clint if there was anything that she could do for him. He thought to himself, "You sure can," but resisted the temptation and thanked her. Elsa was similarly attracted to this tall, handsome, and confident man with a badge.

Clint made it a habit of walking the streets during the day and staying around the bars until midnight. The days were usually uneventful, but once about two weeks after his arrival he saw some action. Paydays were on Fridays, and that's when the bank had a lot of cash on hand. One such Friday, Clint heard a gunshot from the direction of the bank. As he was running to the bank two masked and armed men ran out. Clint yelled, "Stop, hands up!" The bandits turned their guns toward Clint and fired. He felt a bullet graze his arm and take a piece of clothing with it, Clint ducked down behind a water trough, which absorbed a dozen or more shots. He responded by drawing his pistol and peering over the trough. One bandit was mounting his horse and a second was right behind him. Clint fired twice and both dropped. A third bandit exited the bank at high speed. Clint snapped a shot off and the fleeing desperado grabbed his leg and fell to the ground. The lawman cautiously walked up to the bank. Two were dead; one was wounded with a shot in his thigh. Clint recovered the bag with the money and entered the bank. The bank manager was lying on the floor, shot through the heart, and dead. There was no jail or hospital yet, so Clint had the town doc patch up his prisoner as best he could, and a trial was convened in the bar. Nine citizens were chosen from among the bar patrons, and Myron Goodman served as judge, since judicial arrangements had not yet been made for the county. A couple of the jurors had been drinking all day and were unsteady on their feet. They were helped to chairs. There were no lawyers present so Myron ran the show. He called Clint up to stand by him, and made him swear to tell the truth. Clint recounted the events of the day. Myron then asked the defendant if he had anything to say. The man said, "I didn't shoot nobody—it was Billy that shot the man when he pulled out a hidden gun."

The jurors were told to go to the far corner of the room to decide the guilt or innocence of the defendant. Myron asked the foreman if they had reached a verdict. He replied, "Yes, your honor, we find the defendant guilty."

Myron pronounced the sentence: death by hanging:

The bar crowd wasted no time in disposing of the culprit. They marched the man out to the old oak tree and promptly hanged him. It was a joyous occasion for the town. Clever businessmen set up food and drink stands for the spectators, and they made handsome profits.

Clint, disgusted with the carnival atmosphere, went on his way patrolling the town. When his nightly work was done he returned to his home He asked Elsa to heat some water for a bath and then had a relaxed time in the bathroom tub cleaning the dirt and sweat off of himself. After he got into bed there was a knock on the door, and the widow Elsa walked in. "I just wanted to tell you how impressed I am with the way you stopped the bank robbery." She sat on the bed and turned toward Clint. Her robe fell open exposing her naked breasts. She lay down beside Clint and held him to her. Clint helped her out of her robe, and she found his lips and kissed him passionately. When he entered her she exclaimed, "Oh, oh, oh my god, It's been so long." Finally, exhausted by the love making, she clung to him. Clint was conscious of her warm body and delightful scent of perfume.

The sun rose, beginning a new day, and Clint awakened. Elsa was curled around him snugly nestled with her head on his chest. It wasn't possible for Clint to arise without wakening Elsa, and he did so as gently as possible, by kissing her forehead and stroking her hair. When she came to her senses, she wrapped the covers about her and said, "You must think the worst about me, but it has been a terribly long time since I have been intimate with someone."

Clint sat down beside her and responded, "I think you are a wonderful person. We are both in the same boat. It has been a long time for me too. You are a widow and I am a widower. I know what it is to be lonely. Let's just forget this happened, and lead our normal lives."

"Yes, let's do that." Elsa smiled, put on her robe, and left the room.

The arrival of the first train was a cause for a huge celebration in Abilene. A stand had been set up for the dignitaries, and to the right of the stand a place for the band was provided. The band began with a stirring rendition of *The Stars and Stripes Forever* and continued with *Hail Columbia* and *My Country Tis of Thee*. The president of the Kansas Pacific Railway gave a speech about how important the railroad was to Kansas and America, and how a difficult job was completed successfully by his company. Myron then spoke, welcoming the Kansas Pacific Railway to Abilene. This was followed by refreshments and square dancing for those that wanted to. Clint stayed in the shadows watching the crowd for troublemakers and drunkards. On this occasion, there was no trouble.

A hotel for drovers, a stockyard, and stables were built northeast of town to accommodate the cattle drives, and this location was served by a switch allowing Abilene trains to load there.

Soon word spread of the railhead in Abilene, and the town became the destination of cattle drives from Texas and Louisiana. That's when Clint's job began in earnest. Cowboys, who spent months on the trail herding cattle in all sorts of weather, and protecting the cattle from Indians, got paid when the cattle were sold in Abilene, and went out on the town to eat, drink, and be merry.

The construction on Clint's office was amazingly completed in three weeks. It included a jail with two cells and an attached residence with a bedroom, living room with a fireplace, kitchen with a wood cooking stove and hand water pump, a bathroom with bathtub and drain, an attic storage area, and an outhouse. The town had thoughtfully provided basic furniture. When Clint took leave of Elsa, she insisted on straightening up the new residence. When she finished Clint had fresh linens on his bed, towels, dishes, utensils, and an assortment of pots and pans. Most of the items had been contributed by the town, but Elsa found and sorted out all of the items. Before Elsa left, she hugged Clint and gave him a kiss on his cheek, and made the standing invitation for Clint to come to Sunday dinner every week.

Whenever a large herd arrived, a carnival atmosphere prevailed in the town, centered around the bars. On one such evening, Clint heard the report of several gunshots coming out of the Last Hope Saloon. He reached the batwing doors in a rush to find two cowboys lying on the floor. It had been a shootout and both were wounded.

"You go fetch the doc," exclaimed Clint pointing at one of the bar patrons. "What happened here?" asked Clint of the crowd.

"They were fighting over some girl," volunteered one of the bystanders. Clint got a towel from a bartender and tried to staunch the bleeding of one of the injured cowboys. The other one was too far gone to help. It was at this point that Clint decided to ban the carrying of guns in town. The next day he met with Myron who, with some hesitation, agreed to the policy.

At this time, Clint had two deputies. The plan was for one to stay in the office and receive the guns, returning them when the owner was leaving town. The plan worked well, reducing the number of gunshot victims, but some visitors refused to abide with the policy. In these cases, Clint would confiscate the weapon and take the violator to jail, pending payment of a twenty-five-dollar fine.

Clint peered into the dry goods store and waved to the sales clerk and got one in return. Business was good these days as more and more cattle drives came to Abilene. Next door to the dry good's store was the Lucky Seven bar and casino. Gambling was still permitted in Kansas. Clint opened the batwings and saw two cowboys in a poker game sporting six guns. "Please check your guns at the marshal's office across the street."

The taller of the two men replied, "Mister, I never part with my pistol."

"I'm afraid I must insist. They are against the law," responded Clint.

Both cowboys stood up and backed away side by side.

"I guess you'll just have to take them from us."

In the blink of an eye Clint had his pistol out and levels at the two men. "Raise your hands," he said.

The taller cowboy spoke to his partner, "Spread out, circle around him."

Without taking his eyes off the main threat, Clint spoke to the other cowboy, "Take another step and you'll be singing soprano." Clint glanced in the direction of the cowboy to make sure that in stopped moving. Taking advantage of Clint's distraction the tall cowboy pulled at his gun. Clint sensed the draw of the tall cowboy out of the corner of his eye and fired. His bullet landed on the shooting arm of his target and who dropped the half-drawn gun. The other cowboy, amazed at Clint's quick draw and accurate shooting, held his hands up. Clint called for the doc who arrived promptly and applied a bandage, splint, and sling to the wounded cowboy's arm, after dousing it with good whiskey, accompanied by horrible screams.

Clint confiscated the guns and marched the cowboys over to the jail.

Sometimes the cowboys came to Clint for help. One day the foreman of a drive entered the marshal's office. "Marshal, some thieving rustlers helped themselves to about fifty of our cattle last night. Took them right out of the stock pens, they did."

"I'll follow you back to your camp and look into it," responded Clint.

The area around the stockyards was so trampled that finding a trail taken by the rustlers was not possible. The rustlers would need to hide the cattle for a while before attempting to sell them. Clint knew an area in the Flint hills that was ideal for this purpose—a valley rich with grassland hidden by hills, and watered by a creek flowing into the Verdigris River.

Clint rode up the Verdigris River bank and saw tracks made by a herd. He decided to follow the tracks, which led him to the very valley that he had thought the rustlers might have taken the stolen cattle. He mounted a hill that gave him a view over the valley. A shot rang out, striking a rock by Clint. Clint dismounted, pulled his rifle out of the saddle holster, slapped Blackie in his hind quarter to send him down the hill to safety, and found cover behind a flint outcropping. All of this was done swiftly in two seconds.

Several more shots ricocheted off rocks around Clint. From the reports of the shots Clint was able to get a general idea of the direction from where they were coming. He hazarded a quick look. He saw a man about a hundred yards away partially covered behind a flint outcropping. Clint took aim and fired; the shooter went down. Some other shots arrived from either side of Clint. There were at least two other shooters and they were trying to flank him! If he did nothing they would circle around him and shoot him in the back, but to retreat down the hill would expose him to the shooters. Clint had no choice—he ran down the hill to another outcropping, while shots hit all around him. Luckily, Clint was not hit by any of the bullets but felt the sting of chips kicked up by the flying bullets. Under cover again, Clint looked around. One of the men ran from one rock to a second to Clint's left. Clint snapped a shot off, but missed and the man kept running. By the time Clint was ready to shoot again, the man reached his cover. Clint kept his rifle aimed a little above the rock. When the shooter raised himself a little to peer over the rock, Clint shot him right between the eyes. There was now one assailant left, and he chose to run. Clint couldn't shoot him in the back; instead, he ran to Blackie, jumped into the saddle, and chased after the rustler. As he neared the assailant, Clint put a loop in his lariat land threw it over his head. The rustler, a town roustabout by the name of Tom Williams, knew he had had it, and put up no resistance. Clint took Williams gun, gathered up the other guns, and strapped them to one of the horses. The two cadavers were put on two of the other horses with William's help. Knowing that the cattle would not stray far from the lush valley, Clint decided to leave them there, and head to town with his prisoner. Clint returned to the cheers of the cowboys who had lost their cattle.

Clint had been having Sunday dinner with Elsa on a regular basis, and staying the night. The Sunday after his return, Elsa made it clear that she was looking for marriage, and Clint responded that he wasn't ready for that. The Sunday dinner invitations were withdrawn.

Shortly thereafter Myron came to visit him. "Clint I am sorry to say this, but the town council has terminated your employment."

"Why is that Myron? Haven't I done the job exceeding well?"

"You have indeed Clint, but one of the councilman's nephews, Tom Smith, has come to town and is in need of a job—he was previously a lawman. We will give you one month's severance pay."

"Thanks, Myron, I understand. I'll take off tomorrow."

Clint decided to head south to Texas along the Chisholm Trail.

CHAPTER 7

South of Kansas was Indian Territory all the way to Texas. It was prairie land, ideal for the millions of buffalo that roamed the land. Clint saw a large herd in the distance. They were too far away to make out individual animals, but appeared like a moving brown blot painted on the horizon.

Clint kept a wary eye out for Indian raiding parties. They would attack any foreign travelers passing their lands. Acquiring a scalp was a rite of passage for any young brave. The Indians existed on the buffalo, which they used for food and warm clothes. They also made their tepees from buffalo hide.

Clint was startled from the report of rifle shots coming from the direction of the buffalo herd. He urged Blackie forward toward the sounds. Indians did not hunt with guns, but used bow and arrows and spears. These shots were coming from white men. Clint wondered if someone was in trouble. After traveling for about twenty minutes Clint could see a buckboard ahead with two men sitting on the forward seat. One of the men was firing at buffalo, a number of which were lying around dead. A man in dress clothes with a short beard was firing indiscriminately at the buffalo for sport. As Clint got closer, he shouted at the man, "Stop that!" As Clint pulled up to the wagon, the man sitting next to the shooter said, "How dare you! Do you realize that you are shouting at Lord Oxley of Oxbridge."

"I don't care if he is Prince Albert himself. You don't shoot animals that you don't use and leave them lying on the ground!" Lord Oxley did not even look at Clint but continued shooting. Exasperated, Clint grabbed the shotgun out of Oxley's hands and smashed it against the buckboard. The stock shattered. "Do you realize that you just broke a handmade £300 shotgun!"

Oxley now became animated and flushed a deep red, "How dare you, you peasant! Howard, chastise this underclass moron!"

Howard raised a riding crop to whip Clint. As the crop was coming down, Clint grabbed the butler's arm and pulled him out of the buckboard and on to the ground. As Howard started to get up, Clint pulled out his revolver and, pointing it at the butler, said, "Stay down!"

"Oxley, I don't know how you treat people in Britain, but you are in America now and you will respect our rules. There are many Indians and home settlers out here who depend on buffalo to survive. You are welcome to hunt them, but you use what you kill—am I clear?"

Lord Oxley turned away and stared out at the distant landscape. Clint picked up the smashed shotgun and looked for other weapons, and finding none. "You are in danger here from roaming Indians. Let me escort you back to your hotel."

"That won't be necessary. You have done enough damage for one day," replied the butler.

"I insist," responded Clint.

"If you must, come along."

They headed north. After an hour of slow travel limited by the buckboard Clint spotted a cloud of dust to the east. The party continued on its way. Within fifteen minutes, Clint could see that the approaching riders were three braves—probably a raiding group. That became clear when the braves began yelling and shooting their guns at Clint and his fellow travelers. There was little cover except for some tall grass about one hundred feet ahead. Clint pulled Lord Oxley and his butler off of the buckboard and pushed them while unholstering his rifle and leading Blackie into the grass. Bullets whizzed around them, but were inaccurate because the party was well hidden by the grass. Clint refraining from shooting to avoid giving away their location. One of the Indians jumped up on the buckboard and began driving it away. Lord Oxley jumped up and yelled, "They're stealing my buckboard!" Clint advised, "Let them take it—better that than your scalp."

The raiders seemed to be satisfied with the buckboard and left with it. With Lord Oxley and his butler now afoot, the party continued on its way. The pace was not much slower than before. After a full day of traveling, they crossed into Kansas and arrived at the hotel. Clint left, thinking that it would be a long time before Lord Oxley went buffalo shooting again.

CHAPTER 8

Clint headed south again along the Chisholm Trail. Initially all he saw was open prairie as far as the eye could see. As the wind blew the tall grasses, mostly sedge, waved in ripples like water waves in a lake. Although there was new growth grass on this chilly march day, much of the visible grass was last year's grass that remained standing. In this desolate land, Clint's only companion was his horse Blackie—but it was a one-sided conversation.

Up ahead, but as yet far distant, Clint spotted a herd being driven north. He could just make out the drovers on either side of the herd driving them on and containing strays. They must have been on the trail for a month or more, and would probably be dog tired and worn. Clint trotted south to meet the leading elements of the cattle drive. As he got closer, he was surprised to see the condition of the drovers; they were gaunt, trail-worn, and bandaged.

"Howdy, gents," Clint greeted the drovers.

"It's good to see you mister. It's a lonely place on a drive. We must be getting close to civilization," said one of the drovers.

"That you are, sir—about two days north to Abilene," responded Clint.

"Our foreman will want to speak with you. He's about a mile backaways with the wagons."

Clint touched his hat brim and trotted south again.

Cattle were everywhere. Clint thought to himself, "There must be a thousand head of cattle here." He neared three supply wagons and pulled up to the first one, asking the driver, "Howdy, is the trail boss here?"

"He's riding alongside of the wagon behind us," answered the driver.

Clint saw a heavyset man on horse beside the next wagon.

"Howdy, sir, might you be the trail, boss?"

"Why yes, I am, and I am glad to see you! I am looking for some extra help. We got hard hit by an Indian attack two days ago. They killed two of my men and wounded several others. I've got wounded in these wagons instead of supplies. They're still shadowing me, because we drove them off before they could steal more than a handful of steers.

"Sure I'd be happy to, but I might suggest that you leave a hundred head behind to occupy them before they attack you again," responded Clint.

"No, there is no way that I would ever leave those thieving murdering bastards any of my cattle! You are hired right now as drover and security guard, to be paid fifty dollars after the cattle are sold."

"Well, I reckon you have yourself a new hand."

Clint circled around the herd introducing himself to the other hands and discovered who was giving the orders.

They bedded down for the night and Clint was given the midnight to 4:00 AM watch. The job was to circle around the herd and keep them quiet, returning those who wandered away. Clint became fully alert when he heard some owl hoots in two different directions. He checked to see where the other men on watch were and rode over to the nearest one. "Be careful, those are not owls calling—we've got Indians about." Clint had no sooner finished saying that when he heard a gunshot and the cowboy fell from his saddle to the ground. Clint jumped down to check on the wound. That move saved him, as another shot was fired. The cowboy was dead with a bullet through his heart.

Clint pulled his rifle out of its holster and ran with body lowered in the direction of the shot. The cattle were beginning to get spooked by the gun shots. Clint hoped that the other men could keep them quieted down. Just as Clint moved past a couple of steers, he saw dimly an Indian in firing position with one knee on the ground. He was an easy target for a rifle shot, but Clint didn't want to spook the cattle. He pulled his knife from its scabbard and crawled around the Indian, stopping and checking on his foe every minute. When he had reached a point about one hundred yards behind the Indian, he began to close the distance between them—every moment ready to draw his pistol if he were discovered. Finally the moment arrived when he reached about six feet from the shooter, and he lunged for the Indian, pulling back the Indian's jaw with his left hand and slashing the Indian's neck with his right hand. With his carotid artery cut, blood pumped out at a prodigious rate, and the Indian soon went limp. Clint returned to recover his rifle and made the hooting sound. He received a hoot in reply. It came from a distance further away. This time, Clint would use his rifle, and one by one he dispatched the remaining three Indians.

Clint was hailed as a hero in the morning campfire. The herd arrived intact in Abilene, and Clint was paid off with an extra bonus by the trail boss. Now Clint had to decide what to do. Should he stay in Abilene where people knew and respected him, or should he continue on. He was certainly lonely, without his wife or children, no mother or father, and no brothers or sisters. He decided to keep wandering—maybe he would find peace somewhere and someday. He gathered some provisions and headed south back down the Chisholm Trail.

CHAPTER 9

Soon after entering the high plains of the Texas Panhandle, Clint took the Jones-Plummer Trail to Fort Elliot and the nearby town of Sweetwater. Sweetwater, later to be renamed Mobeetie, was a rough and lawless town catering to buffalo hunters and soldiers from Fort Elliot. It had nine saloons, several dancehalls, and was known as a place of prostitution. It was also known for having more than its fair share of bushwhackers and cutthroats.

After checking into Moody's Hotel and getting a bath and shave, Clint left the hotel to take a stroll and get a measure of the town. He became aware that he was being surreptitiously followed. He turned right down a side street and stayed put with his back to a wall. Soon two men with clubs in their hands turned the corner and jumped back with surprise as they saw their quarry waiting for them. Clint rested his hand on the butt of his revolver and asked, "How can I be of service to you two gentlemen?" The two men peered around as if looking for an escape route, and high-tailed out of there.

Clint resumed his stroll and soon heard, "Clint Walker, is that you?" A heavyset man ran up to Clint and said, "Clint, Chet Hendricks from Abilene, do you remember me? You did a terrific job as marshal in Abilene."

"Why yes, I remember you, Chet, you ran, the Lucky Seven saloon."

"Well, I've come to you with a problem Clint. I own the Charging Bull Saloon here in Sweetwater. We have live entertainment, dancing girls who live in upstairs rooms. They dance for free in exchange for room and board. The girls are a great attraction, packing the saloon with big spenders. In between acts, they circulate around the floor, getting men to buy drinks for the girls or themselves. This helps the bottom line. Occasionally, a girl might take a man upstairs. I don't object to it and I take nothing from the girl. They need to make a living too. But more often than not, a girl will get beat up and laid up for a day or a week. That is bad for business. I also feel like a father to these girls and I am hurt when they are. I want to hire you as a security guard."

"You want me to protect prostitutes," responded Clint?

"Yes, and every patron in my saloon. Prostitution is legal in this town. The girls are practicing a legal trade. They don't deserve to be beat up or harmed in any way. I'll pay you top dollar for your services—say twenty-five dollars per week plus you can use a vacant room I have upstairs and have free meals in the kitchen. So what do you say?"

Clint didn't approve of prostitution but knew that there were few choices for uneducated girls who were unmarried—no decent jobs and an impoverished life in a spinning mill. He didn't have anything to do at this point in his journey, so he responded, "It's a deal."

Clint walked over to the Charging Bull Saloon with Chet. On the way, they passed groups of rough looking inebriated men trying to stay upright as they sang bawdy songs or told jokes. In this town most men were either drunk or were going to get drunk. The Charging Bull Saloon was half full of men standing at the bar, playing poker at a table, or gambling at craps, roulette, or the blackjack station. Clint noticed three girls circulating in the main saloon area. Chet introduced Clint to the two bartenders, three gamers, three girls, two kitchen staff, and the back room banker. He was then taken up to his room, which seemed comfortable enough. Clint then took his leave as he saw to the stabling and care of Blackie. When he returned, he went up to his room and discovered that there were four girls living upstairs. None of the women were what you would call beautiful, but each one had a certain flair that made them desirable. Ginger was a redhead with a wasp figure and hazel eyes. Dorothy had beautiful upturned hair and looked matronly. Monica had a large bosom and a vixen facial expression. Nancy was the most attractive of the four with rosy cheeks, inviting red lips, an ample bosom, thin waste, and a teasing look about her.

Clint took a two hour nap and then, feeling refreshed, went down to the saloon floor. After walking around to get a feel for the place and its patrons, he stationed himself by the stairs. Occasionally one of the girls would lead a patron upstairs. Clint's attention was captured by some loud yelling at one of the poker tables. A burly whiskered buffalo hunter was arguing with another player. "You damn cheat, I want my money back," shouted the big man! The other man was slight of build and dressed in a black suit. Clint walked quickly over to the table. As the burly man moved to grab the other, the slight man whipped out a pistol in a lighting draw. Clint yelled, "Hold on there!" Reaching the table, he pushed the gun arm down and said, "What's the problem here?"

"That man is pulling cards out of his clothes," said the buffalo hunter. Clint spoke to the card sharp, "Holster your gun mister." He complied. Clint felt the sleeve of the card sharp and pulled out an ace of spades. "Looks like you were cheating. Get going and leave your money on the table."

The card sharp backed away and challenged Clint, "Draw when you're ready." From the back of the saloon, someone yelled, "Don't do it, mister, that's Black Bart, and he's killed ten people so far!"

Clint responded to the card sharp, "Now you draw when you're ready." What happened next became long talked about in the west. Black Bart began his lightening draw, but before he could clear his holster, Clint had his weapon out and pointed at him. Black Bart froze, waiting for the impact of the bullet. Clint then quietly said, "Clear out, mister," and reholstered his pistol.

Black Bart turned and walked for the exit. When he reached the batwings he turned, gun in hand and pointed at Clint. Clint drew his pistol so fast that no one saw his hand move until the gun was in his hand. They fired simultaneously. Bart's shot took a piece of clothing off Clint's ribs and smashed into the wall. Clint's shot was true. It slammed into Bart's chest and through his heart. Bart would not again see the light of day.

Clint was beginning to get weary of a life of working most of the night and sleeping whenever he found some time. One evening when things were quiet, Clint went up to his room to catch a short nap. He was awakened by some screams. Jumping up he ran to the source of the screams. They were coming from the room next door—Nancy's room. Nancy was one of Clint's favorite girls. He saw an already battered and bruised girl being choked by a big guy sitting on top of her in bed. Moving quickly, Clint put a choke hold around the guy's neck and pulled back. The man had no choice but to fall back and release his hold on the girl. He was one of the biggest men that Clint had ever seen. The man threw himself back on to the floor, landing on top of Clint, and causing Clint to expel his breath and release his hold on the man, who got up and kicked Clint in the ribs. Clint felt a sharp pain in his ribs, and he struggled to get up. Once up, Clint was hit on his left cheek by a sledgehammer blow that knocked Clint back on the floor as his head went spinning. Clint did not want another kick in his already broken ribs, so he pulled his bowie knife out and held it in front of his ribs. The kick came, more powerful than the first, but before landing, the man's shin was pierced by the knife, which travelled around the fibia and slashed open the adductor muscle of the thigh. The man screamed with pain, fell to the floor, and held his profusely bleeding leg. Clint found one of Nancy's nightgowns and wrapped it around the man's wound. Nancy ran over to Clint, wrapped her arms around him and said, "Oh Clint, thank you! I thought he was going to kill me." Clint took a look at her and said, "Your face is pretty beat up—let me wash it for you." Ignoring the moaning man on the floor, Clint found the pitcher and basin, and wiped the blood off of Nancy's face with a towel. "Does he owe you any money," he asked?

"Yes, eight dollars." she answered.

"With the nightgown, beating, and towel we'll make it twenty." Clint walked to the moaning man, went through his pockets, and found a twenty-dollar gold coin that he gave to Nancy.

"Clint get into bed with me, I owe you some thanks." Clint declined politely. He had gotten many offers from the girls, but had refused everyone, not only because of his moral compass, but also knowing how jealousy and gossip spread in a place like this.

Clint decided that the time had come to wander on. The schedule of working at night in a loud and smoke filled saloon and sleeping during the day had made him weary and longing for the great outdoors.

Chet Hendricks was, of course, upset to learn of Clint's decision but made a good face about it and even gave Clint a going away party. Throughout the evening, the girls clung to Clint and wished him well. The next morning they all made it a point to be up to see him off. Clint mounted Blackie and headed south.

CHAPTER 10

Clint Walker stared at the vast fields of bluebonnets ahead as he entered the Texas hill country of Bastrop County. His black saddle-bred sensed the river ahead and perked her ears up at the thought of a refreshing drink after a long morning's ride. Clint rode ahead to the Colorado River and let his horse drink and graze a while. He thought he would ride southeast along the river and then make camp before sundown. A Captain in Confederate General J. E. B. Stuart's Calvary, Clint had seen his last battle at the debacle at Sailor's Creek, just before the surrender at the Appomattox Court House. Clint was allowed to keep his side arm and horse, but had to turn in his Sharp muzzle-loader carbine. He did, however, manage to find his Spencer repeating cartridge rifle, which he had captured from a Yankee at Yellow Tavern and subsequently hid in the root cellar of a Richmond townhouse that had escaped the war. He now carried that Spencer in his saddle holster. Ammunition for the long gun, impossible to find in the South during the war, was now available in most general stores throughout the West.

When Clint had returned to his Kentucky home after the surrender, he was horrified to discover that his wife had died of Cholera months before, and his home had been burned to the ground. Feeling lost, he set out with no particular destination in mind. For a while he lived in Kansas and held a job as a town marshal, and later as a cowhand. Forever restless, he then travelled south along the Chisholm Trail, passing herds being driven north to Kansas railheads. The cold and snows of March were now behind him, and this April morning was sunny and mild.

After a few hours, Clint noticed some grazing cattle here and there, telling him that he was entering a cattle ranch. It seemed ideal for that purpose—the river providing plenty of fresh water and the pasture land with lush green grass for grazing.

The trail took Clint over a hill, from where he could see a ranch house in the distance. As he neared the house he could make out some people seemingly raising a ruckus. He increased his speed to a canter. There was a carriage with a man in a black suit, and another man wrestling with a woman in a blue dress and bonnet. Some of the contents of the house were lying on the ground in front of the house. He heard a woman's voice yelling, "Let me go!" Things sort of got frozen as they noticed Clint was near. Clint said, "What's the matter here?" The man in the black suit responded. "Stay out of this, mister. We are serving an Writ of Eviction for failure to pay taxes due." The woman screamed, "This carpet bagger owns everything in town. He sets outrageous taxes, and when they aren't paid, he takes the property. I can pay the tax in Confederate money, the only kind we made during the war, but he won't accept it." Clint looked back at the black-suited man. "I don't set the tax rates—they are set by the governor-general of the forces of occupation."

"I assume you can prove that the tax money goes directly to the governor-general," responded Clint, who then added, "Let me see that Writ of Eviction." Clint eyed the paper that was handed to him and said, "Mister, this paper must be signed by a judge. It appears to have only your name as signatory. It's not worth the match to burn it."

"Why, no one has ever questioned my right to do that as the designated tax authority in the county."

"Sorry, mister, now clear out!"

The hombre holding the woman let her go and faced Clint in the gun-draw position.

"You are not going to tell us what to do, stranger!"

Clint responded, "Well, don't bore me—draw or clear out!" The man hesitated a bit, then relaxed and said, "We'll be back for sure—you can count on that, stranger!"

The man mounted his horse and followed the carriage with the black-suited man as it left the ranch. The woman, who Clint thought was mighty pretty, said, "I'm Anne Williams. My husband died at Gettysburg. I have tried to keep the ranch operating, but then that carpetbagger Lloyd Bagget arrived as tax collector and started taking over everything in Bastrop. He scared away all of my hands, and I don't know what I am going to do." Clint responded, "Well, ma'am, I'll try to keep a look-out on your ranch, but I'll be drifting on before long. Do you have any family here about that could help?"

"No, I'm afraid not—my family is in Louisiana, and their home got destroyed by the Yankees."

"Let me help you get your furniture back in the house." Clint pushed, dragged, and carried all of the furniture that had been removed by the interlopers back into the house. He was offered a meal, which he accepted, and then sat in a rocking chair on the porch, while Anne did wonders in the kitchen. The meal was beefsteak, fried potatoes, and garden greens, followed by apple pie. "Ma'am, this is about the best and biggest meal I have had in many years, and I am much obliged."

Clint liked the way Anne's curly hair fell over her left eye, and the way she absent-mindedly brushed it back. Clint rode out on the road to town, but when he was out of sight, he doubled around and made dry camp on the hilltop overlooking the ranch house. The next morning Clint made a dugout several feet below the apex of the hill and stood watch. A cloud of dust in the distance told him that several riders were approaching the ranch house at a fast clip. When they arrived they fired their pistols at the house, lassoed and tore down the corral, and were about to set the bunk house on fire when Clint let fly with his Spencer. Clint downed three of the eight outlaws before they realized that they were under fire. In the exchange of gunfire that followed, two more outlaws fell, while their fire was wide of the mark. The remaining outlaws retreated down the road, hell bent for leather.

Clint rushed down to the house to check on the woman. He entered the house through the front door. Anne was standing there with a rifle in her arms. "Are you okay?" Clint asked.

"I'm fine. I stayed away from the windows when they shot up the house."

"I'm mighty glad you didn't shoot me when I barged in here." Clint declined the offered breakfast. He checked the downed outlaws—four were dead and one had a broken arm and was bleeding profusely. Clint dressed the wound to stop the bleeding, and found some sticks to splint the arm.

He borrowed Anne's wagon and horses, loaded the dead and wounded, and started into town—hitching his horse to the back of the wagon. Clint knew that the harassment wasn't going to stop so long as Bagget was around.

His entrance into town caused a commotion when the citizenry noticed Clint's cargo.

He got directions to the sheriff's office, and explained what happened, using Anne's name as a witness. The Sheriff was sympathetic, saying he couldn't move against Bagget because he was protected by the captain of the occupying Union Army. That information raised the suspicion in Clint's mind that Bagget and the Captain were in cahoots together to steal the money and properties of the people in the county.

Bagget worked in the county land assessment office. When Clint entered, he saw Bagget at a desk in a private room and a single clerk at a desk in the reception area. "Mr. Bagget, I've come to see your records of tax money transfers to the State and County Governments."

"I'm sorry, whoever you are, we don't provide them to the public."

"Well, I'm going over to the county headquarters and find out from them. I'll be back."

At the county office, Clint discovered that Bagget was keeping over 20 percent of the county taxes for himself. Clint walked back to the land office, and found Bagget outside, flanked by two gunslingers, waiting for him. "Whoever you are, mister, you are a troublemaker, and we are taking you to the Army Office for questioning."

"Bagget, you are a thief, extortionist, and dirty liar, and I'm going nowhere with you."

"You're outnumbered mister, drop your gun belt and we won't harm you."

"You may get me—but one thing's for sure—you are my first target Bagget."

Bagget, suddenly looking nervous, yelled, "Draw!"

In the smallest fraction of a second, before Bagget and the gunslingers could clear leather, Clint had drawn and shot each of the three in the chest, and through the heart. The Sheriff had been on his way over and had witnessed the fight—declaring that Clint had acted in self-defense.

Clint returned to the ranch in the wagon, trailing his horse from behind. As he got to the ranch house, Anne rushed out and yelled, "You're back! I was so worried."

Clint noticed how beautiful she looked and he responded, "I understand that you are looking to hire ranch hands, and I'm applying!"

CHAPTER 11

Anne looked at Clint, brushed her hair back, and smiled, "You're hired as my foreman, mister, but I have to pay you in Confederate money until we make some Yankee dollars."

"That will be fine," Clint responded. He knew that he would need to hire some ranch hands; he couldn't run the ranch by himself. He had saved some money from his days of wandering, and he could use this money for immediate ranch needs. There were about five hundred head of cattle on the ranch. They needed to take about four hundred steers to the Kansas railhead for sale, leaving the breeding stock behind. That would give them necessary income to keep the ranch in operation.

Clint checked the area around the ranch house. The bunkhouse had survived the morning's attack unscathed. There were bunks for eight hands, a storeroom for saddles and tackle, two wood-burning stoves, and a kitchen with canned goods, a cook's fireplace, and table with chairs. He claimed a bunk and stowed his meager possessions in the trunk at the foot of his bunk.

Clint then took leave of Anne to travel to Austin, where they had telegraph service. He quickly packed his things and left on the trail to Austin. The trail passed through a forest of loblolly pines—the last remnant of an ancient forest of these trees that once covered the entire state. The fresh pine smell was invigorating. The trail took a WSW course, roughly following the Columbia River. By noon Clint was in the outskirts of Austin. He saw a telegraph pole and followed it into the city to the telegraph office. Once there, he wrote out a message to Matt Walker, "Need help running Double Bar ranch near

Bastrop Texas stop Round up gang and come down stop." These were men who served with Clint in Confederate General J .E. B. Stuart's Calvary and who would most likely be looking for jobs. While waiting for help, Clint kept busy. He did what he could by himself. He rebuilt the corral, which had been torn down by the Bagget gang when he had first arrived, did minor repairs on the bunkhouse and stable, and stacked hay and firewood for the winter. Clint then travelled around the range to do a tally of the herd. The results were both disappointing and alarming. Clint's return trip was uneventful, but he worried that he didn't see the usual number of steers on the Double Bar Range. He counted eighty-five head and thirty calves of a prior herd of five hundred. There was some rustling taking place! He would have to wait for the hands to arrive before he could chase after the stolen cattle.

He would have to wait for the hands to arrive before he could chase after the stolen cattle.

Jake LaMatta took the red-hot branding iron and seared the hide of the prone steer. The branding iron changed the double bar that looked like an equal sign (=) into a z and added another z so the double bar brand became a double z—the brand of a now-defunct ranch owned by one of the men. There was the usual bellow of pain and a rush to return to the herd after the ties were removed. This was hard work, but not as hard as raising the beef themselves. When Jake and his four buddies had arrived at Bastrop after robbing the bank in Houston, they had heard about a spread with five hundred cattle run by a widow without any cowhands. Although they had the bank money, this was too easy an opportunity to pass up. There was also the bonus of having their way with the widow. So they rounded up all the cattle they could find—about four hundred head—and drove them to the hill country, fresh with tall spring grass. They couldn't find the widow. After they fattened the steers up, they would drive them up to the Chisholm Trail and, hopefully, sell them to a passing herder before arriving in Kansas City.

Clint was outside holding a skein of yarn for Anne while she was sewing a blouse together when Matt Walman, Jess Harding, Jim Early, and Clyde Farrar rode up to the ranch house. Matt, who had ridden with Clint throughout the war, smiled and said, "Boys, it looks like Clint has finally found something he's good at." There were handshakes and greetings all around. Clint took them to the bunkhouse and got the cowboys squared away as he explained the situation. Later in the day, the group rode around the range to assess the situation. In the northeast sector of the pastureland, Jess spoke up, "Hey, guys, look at all this grass that's been trampled down. A herd was driven through here." A herd of four hundred cattle deposits a lot of scat as it travels. The cowboys followed the trail of scat into the hill country. Clyde complained, "I never don realized that I would get ever get a job as a scat follower." Jess answered, "Clyde, you're lucky that we don't have to harvest the stuff."

As they reached the summit of the hill, a lush green pastureland appeared to them. They saw the stolen cattle surrounded by a half dozen men on horseback. Clint said, "We'll drive down on them, maybe stampede the cattle, and pick 'em off. Form up! The cavalry men came to attention five abreast in attack position. Clint then gave the order, "Forward, charge!" The horses leaped as one as the troop thundered down the hill, six guns firing, and the men screaming the rebel yell. Clint chose to use his sword instead of his sidearm. The rustlers, caught off guard, panicked at the sight of the charging horsemen, and took off as fast as they could—that is, except for the unfortunate ones who got in the way of the stampeding herd and were trampled.

The troop split up and chased after the escaping rustlers. In the end, one of the rustlers was killed by the stampeding herd and another was injured, one was killed by the troopers and two surrendered. A search of the saddlebags found the stolen bank money. They made the wounded rustler as comfortable as possible for someone suffering from multiple broken bones and hog-tied the others. The rest of the day was spent rounding up the scattered herd. The men bedded down the cattle and made camp while Clint headed into town.

Clint tried to calm himself as he headed down the trail to Bastrop. The surrounding land was made beautiful by a profusion of spring wildflowers—purple phlox, violet wisteria, blue sage, yellow buttercup, and red-orange corn poppy. Here and there, patches of sweet alyssum gave off a sweet honey fragrance. Clint passed by stands of woods with elm, oak, palmetto, and pine trees. As he neared town, he passed more than a few homes and small farms. Clint pulled up at the sheriff's office. A deputy said that the sheriff was across the street at the Royal Tavern having lunch. Clint walked over and through the bat wings at the entrance. He entered into a tense situation.

The sheriff, his back to the bar, was facing some Circle C hands, and calmly said, "Come on, Butch, I have a warrant for your arrest. We'll sort things out at my office." Butch and three other Circle C hands were crouched in a draw position. "Sheriff, he ain't going nowhere—now git!" spoke Casey Legere, one of the Circle C hands. The Circle C was the largest spread in the county, and its hands tended to ride roughshod over anyone in town. Butch was a bully who had beaten an elderly storekeeper to a pulp for running out of chewing tobacco.

Clint was careful to separate himself physically from the sheriff. He said, "I'd take it as unfriendly for any Circle C to draw his gun."

"You stay out of this cowpoke, it ain't none of your business," replied Butch.

"Hey, you," said Clint, pointing at Butch with his left hand. "Have you eaten lunch yet?"

"Yah, why do you ask?"

Clint, smiling, responded, "I sure hate to belly-shoot some-one with a full stomach. It gets messy. You know what I mean—all that goo! Kind of greenish and smells worse that a whore's backside. Whatever your buddies do, I will get at least one shot out into your belly. If I were you, I'd just go along with the sheriff."

Butch, thinking things over, decided to back down. "All right, Sheriff, I'll go . . . but I ain't don nothing wrong."

Clint decided to walk back to the jail with the sheriff. After the sheriff had locked Butch in a cell, Clint set down next to the sheriff's desk and tossed a saddlebag on top of it. "Jim, there's fifteen thousand dollars there in freshly printed new bills. Judging by the wrappers, I'd say it came from the First National Bank of Houston. We took them off some rustlers we caught up with."

Sheriff Jim Walker smiled and said, "Clint, I want to thank you for backing my play at the saloon. I felt sure that I was going to eat lead in there until you arrived. I owe you one. The First National Bank of Houston was robbed yesterday morning by six men. A bank teller was murdered. Do you have these men in custody?"

"One is dead, one wounded, and the other three no worse for wear."

"Good," responded the sheriff. "The bank put up a $500 reward on each of them, dead or alive. I'll send a deputy to Austin to wire the bank and get their instructions on paying the reward. Meanwhile, I'll return with you to take this gang into custody and charge them with rustling."

The next morning, the sheriff, two deputies, and Clint set out to recover the rustlers. One of the deputies drove a spring suspension wagon to transport the rustlers. The wounded man would see a doctor, if he survived the trip, when they returned to town. Clint went with the sheriff, but he ordered his men to herd the cattle back to their range. It was rough going for the wagon until they reached the trail. The wounded rustler moaned with each jolt of the wagon. After the miscreants had been jailed, Clint joined the sheriff with a cup of coffee. "I have good news for you, Clint. The bank instructed me to pay the reward money with the recovered cash, so I'll give you $2,500 before you leave, and a deputy to guard you on your return if you like."

"Jim, I'll be glad for the cash, but will decline with my thanks your offer of a deputy."

Clint left early the next morning, after spending the night at the Bastrop Inn. By midday he reached the ranch house. Anne ran out to greet him and was unrestrained in the enthusiasm of her greeting. With her arms around his neck, she said, "My returning hero, don't wiggle, I am going to kiss you!" She did, and Clint liked it and kissed her again.

"Men," Clint addressed the team, "so far it's been no picnic being here. I want you to know how much Miss Anne and I appreciate you answering the call. Now there was a reward we got for turning in those rustlers, and we'll share it equally—$500 apiece."

"Wahoo!" yelled Clyde. "That there's a whole year's pay! I'll trail cow dung every day for that kind of money!" Clint counted out four piles of $500 and presented the money to each of the ranch hands. "It's good to have some Yankee money that can be spent," said Jess Harding. The next day was spent preparing for the roundup and drive to the Kansas City railhead. Clint took the wagon into town for supplies—some for Anne, and most for the chuck wagon. They would take cans of beans, sides of bacon, bags of cornmeal, and ammunition. Clint had his Spencer repeating rifle and a Colt .45 pistol. The men each had sidearms.

While Clint was gone the men spent the day separating out the cattle to stay from those that would leave. Clint assigned Clyde the job as wagon driver and cook. At sunup the group began moving the cattle out. The weather had turned hot and humid, and the going was made difficult by the heat and dust. By dusk they had reached the trail north and bedded the herd down for the evening. Clint went hunting with his long gun and returned with a small deer and two rabbits. Two men were always on watch with the cattle, and the others sat around the fire eating and joking. At nightfall they slept, using their saddles as pillows. And so they continued on day after day. Every water crossing was an opportunity for the cattle to drink and for the men to wash up. They averaged about twelve miles each day, stopping to let the cattle graze every now and then. The measured pace kept the weight on the cattle and gave needed rest to the horses and men. A new railhead with holding pens had just opened in Abilene Kansas, and that would be their destination. One evening, just before bedding the herd down, Clint heard the rumble of thunder to the west. He led the men in quickly bedding down the herd and splitting to them up and circling them. Suddenly the storm struck, shafts of lightening lit the sky, blasts of thunder made ear-shattering crescendos of trumpeting noise, and torrents of windblown rain came down on them. The cattle, scared witless, were ready to stampede, but the men kept circling and talking. They had to keep the first one from bolting because the others would follow. Then it happened. A brilliant flash of lightning, accompanied by an ear-crushing clap of thunder, descended on them. The entire herd, as one, took off in a stampede. Clint, who was on break, jumped on to his horse and joined the others in trying to stem the running herd. Rain came down in sheets, restricting visibility even further in the dark night. More from sound than sight, the cowboys rode ahead of the cattle and began the process of turning them. If smartly done, the cattle would form a circle and eventually tire from running. This was accomplished.

Morning brought sun and a freshness in the air. Clint reckoned that the stampede had cost them about a dollar a head in lost weight. A group of about ten cowboys came upon them from the direction of Abilene. The leader of the group approached Clint and said, "We'll drive those steers into Abilene for you and buy them from you on the spot." Clint responded, "How much are you offering?" The cowboy looked over the herd and said, "Well, ya know, we just sold a herd in Abilene and didn't get but $12 a head. They've got plenty of beef now and won't offer even that much. We'll take a chance and give you $10 a head."

"We were hoping for $20 a head, but will settle now for $16." The cowboy chuckled, turned away, and swung back holding a six-shooter in his hand pointed at Clint's midsection. "We'll just take them off your hands. How's that, mister?" Clint saw that the cowboy's sidekicks had also drawn their weapons and had them pointed at his men. "You're good—I'll give you that," said Clint as he raised his hands midlevel. I'll tell you what, I'll buy them back from you," said Clint as he pulled a big wad of bills from his pocket. He reached toward the cowboy with the bills to hand them over, but as the cowboy moved his left hand to accept the bills, Clint dropped them. As the cowboy's attention was momentarily diverted to the falling cash, Clint grabbed the cowboy's gun hand, twisted, and pulled the gun away as he put his opponent in a hammerlock, hugging him with his back toward his partners, and with Clint holding a gun to his head. "Drop your guns!" yelled Clint, "or I start shooting—you first, then your boss." Clint jerked the cowboy's arm up, causing terrible pain, as he said to the cowboy, "Tell them."

"Drop your guns, dammit!" yelled the cowboy. Clint's men then gathered up the thieves' gun, and had them raise their hands.

Clint released his hostage and then exploded a haymaker to his jaw that sent him sprawling on the ground. "All right, get out of here! We will keep your guns. Don't even think of coming back."

Clint and his four hands made Abilene with the herd in another two weeks. Clint found a buyer for the herd at $20 a head, for a total of a little over $8,000. Each of the men was paid $40, and counting the reward money, they were well stocked. It was a wild town, filled with bars, brothels, burlesque shows, and thieves, so Clint insisted that the group stick together. They enjoyed hot baths, shaves, shows, whiskey, and women.

The trip home took only three weeks. Anne ran out to welcome them and gave Clint a big hug. After Clint and the men had taken baths and changed clothes, they ate, and the men rested outside the bunk house singing ballets while the sun went down. Clint went in the house with the proceeds to settle the account with Anne. "Why, I don't think I have ever seen so much money in my life," said Anne. Twirling her hair above her left eye, and shyly glancing at Clint, she said, "It sure would be nice to share it with someone—maybe a cowboy who isn't too shy to pop the question." Clint turned to her, gathered her into his arms, and looked into her beautiful blue eyes, and said, "My darling Anne, maybe I am too shy, but I know I love you and want to care for you, cherish you, and make you mine. I promise to love you always—will you marry me?" Anne smiled as she moved closer into his embrace and said coyly, "Let me think about it a second—the second is up! I most definitely will have, hold, love, and obey you, until death do us part, my darling Clint. Do we have to wait for a preacher before we do something about it?" she said, as she led him into the bedroom.

CHAPTER 12

Ernesto D'ablio sat patiently overlooking a ranch house from a hill about a mile away. With him were ten hombres in his gang of desperados. They had come north from Mexico to rape and steal. It was exciting to think of all of the treasure that awaited them. Finally the day gave way to a moon lit night. The light from the ranch house window was extinguished. Ernesto waited another hour to let the couple go to sleep and then ordered his men to move quietly forward. They tethered their horses and walked silently up to the door of the ranch house.

The door was unlocked, as expected in this part of Texas. They entered and crept into the bedroom. Ernesto pulled out his revolver and shot the man in the head. The sound of the gun firing awoke the woman who saw them and screamed a mighty cry. The men took the woman out of the room while Ernesto searched for valuables. She continued to scream until the men were finished and one of them used a knife to end the noise. Ernesto found a jar with some coins of silver and gold, a silk man's shirt, a belt with a silver buckle, and a woman's fancy dress. His men went through the kitchen and took silverware, utensils, and china. Further search resulted in a rifle and revolver with belt and holster. They took whatever food they could find and went to the stable, where they found two horses and tackle.

This was a thoroughly successful raid, thought Ernesto. He would continue on to Bastrop where they would get drunk and party. They continued on, using the stolen horses to carry their booty. The trail to Bastrop led to a wooden bridge that spanned the Colorado River. When Ernesto reached the other side, he noticed a large herd of cattle to his right. Whoever owned those cattle must be very rich, at least by Mexican standards! So Ernesto decided to delay their celebration in Bastrop and look for the ranch house that went with the cattle. They turned to the right and wandered along the riverbank.

They saw a hill and decided to climb it to look around. When they reached the summit, they saw a ranch house. The moon still shone brightly. There were no lights in the ranch house. They descended from the hill toward the ranch house.

Clint had had a hard day. He and the men had rounded up the calves for branding and castration. There were scores of the young beeves. Since there was a full moon the men worked into the late afternoon to finish up, and then had dinner at nightfall. The job now completed, they headed back to the ranch to get some sleep.

As Clint neared the ranch house, he saw some movement on the hill, and wondered what it was. When they got closer, Clint saw that the movement was a group of men on horseback. There was no reason at this time of night for a band of men to be about. Clint raised his hand and said, "Men, there's a suspicious group ahead. We must intercept them before they get to the ranch house. Anne is all alone there. Get ready to charge, and be prepared for anything! In line. Now forward charge! " This was second nature to the men who had served in JEB Stuart's cavalry. They were outnumbered five against ten, but they were very good at this sort of thing.

The Mexicans awoke to the charging cowboys. Clint saw a man who appeared to be the leader urging his men forward to meet the charge, while he continued on to the ranch house. Clint, urging Blackie to speed ahead, veered toward the ranch house. To his dismay, he saw the Mexican enter. With reckless disregard for whatever obstacles might be before him in the moon lit night, Clint rode faster and faster. As he arrived at the front door, he heard Anne scream. Finally in the bedroom he saw a figure standing over Anne with a knife. The man turned to face Clint and attacked with the knife. Clint fended off the knife with his left arm while he delivered a lightening punch with his right fist to the assailants jaw. The man screamed in pain. Clint twisted the knife out of the Mexican's hand, and delivered a flurry of punches to the man's body and head. He continued until the Mexican dropped down unconscious.

Clint, resisting the temptation to use the fallen knife on the Mexican, lifted Anne up to hug her and asked, "Are you okay, my darling?"

"Yes, my wonderful knight, just a little shaken."

"No one will ever get that close to you again. I promise!"

Clint had shut his mind to the gunfire outside. He let go of Anne and ran to the door. In the initial charge three of the bandits had been wounded and unhorsed by the accurate shooting of the ranch hands. Three of the remaining six had galloped away, and three had taken refuge in the bunkhouse and were now exchanging gunfire with the cowboys. Clint ran to the back of the bunkhouse and inched his way around to an open window. He saw the bandits firing from the front door; without hesitation, Clint poured bullets into the bandits. It didn't matter that he took them from behind. He didn't care.

The final score was three dead or dying, four captured, including the ringleader, two with bullet wounds but would survive, and three who escaped. The cowboys found the two stray horses packed with loot.

The prisoners were hogtied and left in the stable. Clint and the ranch hands were plumb exhausted, but took turns on watch in case the escaped bandits returned. In the morning the dead, the prisoners, and the loot were transported to Bastrop and turned over to Sheriff Walker.

CHAPTER 13

Clint sat at a table in the Royal Tavern with his back to the wall nursing a beer. He had come into town as a prosecution witness at the trial of the Mexican banditos who had attacked the Double Bar a week ago. When they would be found guilty, and Clint was sure they would be, justice would be swift. One of the few community events that pleased the public was a hanging. A festive atmosphere would prevail, and vendors would sell sandwiches and pies to a celebrating public.

Clint planned on returning to the Double Bar tomorrow. A few bar girls were working the patrons. One had approached Clint but he wasn't interested. His heart was completely captured by Anne, and he would never break his marriage vows. The saloon was noisy with a large crowd letting off steam. Suddenly an angry argument broke out and Clint heard loud challenges spoken. The two men involved were not known to Clint, so he ignored it. A hush broke out as the men faced each other for a duel with six-guns. They were uncomfortably close. Clint did not want to be hit by a stray bullet, so he got up and stepped between the men with his arms outstretched and said, "Back off, men, not here, not now."

"Stay out of this, mister, it ain't none of your business," was what Clint heard. In a lightening movement that spectators would later swear they did not see, Clint grabbed the shirt of the man to his right and tossed him into the man on his left. They both tumbled to the ground. Quick as a wink Clint drew his pistol and held it over the two men. "What is the problem here," he asked?

"He shoved me at the bar," one of the men responded.

"I tell you what, there's plenty of elbow room at the bar now. Have a drink on me," said Clint. "Shake hands first."

The three men ponied up to the bar and Clint ordered a round of whisky drinks.

All was going well, the two men had cooled down, when Clint heard some shots coming from the direction of the jail. Clint excused himself and ran outside. He was met with gunfire from the formerly imprisoned Mexicans. Clint didn't have a chance. He took two slugs—one in his left arm, one in his left leg. Although no major blood vessel was severed, the bleeding was substantial, and his humorous was fractured. Clint heard people yelling, "He killed the sheriff, get him!" And from a prone position, he drew his gun and fired back—hitting two of the banditos with fatal shots. By this time the outlaws were mounted and the leader yelled at Clint, "We get your woman now!" Clint, in great pain, crawled to his horse and mounted him after a couple of tries. He said, "Go home, Blackie," and led his horse toward the Double Bar. Clint travelled as quickly as the pain in his arm would allow. After a while, he stopped and fashioned a sort of sling from his bandana. That helped some.

The ranch hands had eaten their evening meal and were settling into their bunks when the two bandits burst into the bunkhouse with drawn guns. In the ensuing gun battle, three of the four hands were shot—two fatally, Jim Early, and Clyde Farrar, while only Matt Waltman emerged unscathed. One of the two bandits was killed, but the leader, Ernesto D'ablio, ducked out, leaving his companion to receive the flying bullets.

Matt ran after the bandit who was heading to the ranch house where Anne resided.

It was fortunate that Blackie knew the way home because Clint blacked out for a period from loss of blood. As he neared the ranch house he saw Matt chasing the bandit who was heading to the ranch house. Spurring Blackie on, he got between the bandit and the house. His pistol spoke twice and Ernesto crumpled to the ground.

Although Ernesto was severely wounded, Clint, after learning about the carnage in the bunkhouse, decided to hang the outlaw before he died of his wounds. A noose was hung from the oak tree and put around Ernesto's neck. He was slowly raised up and chocked to death, as he struggled in his death throes. Justice in the west was not always pretty, but Ernesto would rape and kill no more.

CHAPTER 14

Clint Walker's mood changed from somber to ebullient as he viewed the beauty of the hills bright with the colors of wild flowers—yellow daisies, pink columbines, and blue violets. It was his second spring in the Texas hill country, and he was returning to his beautiful wife, Anne, who was far along in her pregnancy, and would soon give him an heir. The ranch came into view as soon as he crossed the Colorado River. In twenty minutes, he would be home. His trip to Austin had been successful. The bank had agreed to extend them a sizable loan, which would enable them to vastly expand the ranch operation.

As Clint pulled up to the ranch house, Melita, their live-in maid rushed out and yelled, "Mr. Clint, the time has come for the baby." Clint ran into the house and to their bedroom. Anne was in labor. He kissed her in greeting and ran to get Matt, who he sent rushing to town to get the doctor. Clint stayed with Anne who was having a rough time.

In what seemed to be an eternity, Doc Simpson arrived with his medical bag. As he rushed into the bedroom, he called out to Melita for a pan of hot water and a half dozen towels. Clint felt helpless. He walked outside and sat on the porch chair. He tried to close his ears to the sounds he heard until they changed into screams and much commotion. Was their baby okay? Dear God, let Anne be well!

After a half hour, Doc Simpson came out. "Clint, steel yourself now. The baby boy was still born. It was a difficult breech birth, and your wife developed a hemorrhage. She didn't make it."

Clint felt like he had been punched in the gut. He reeled backward and fell to the floor. "Oh my god, no no!" He got up and slowed walked into the bedroom, past the bloody towels to his dead wife. He didn't see his baby. He bent over, and with tears dropping from his eyes, kissed Anne good-bye. He then asked the doc to find Matt and ask him to come. When Matt arrived, he said, "Clint, I can't tell you how sorry I am. Is there anything I can do?"

Clint responded, "Matt, please arrange for a Christian burial for my wife and child. I have written out this deed transferring the ranch to you."

At the appointed day the church in town was packed in tribute to Anne and Clint. The precession walked to the church cemetery, and Anne and the baby were laid to rest. Clint mounted Blackie, and headed north out of town, with no particular destination in mind . . . Just wandering.

CHAPTER 15

Clint headed north into Indian Territory. In two weeks, he entered high plains of the newly established territory of Colorado. He marveled at the beauty of the San Luis Valley nestled between the Sangre De Christo and the San Juan Mountains. He decided to stop in the town of Leadville. Recent silver finds had populated the town with prospectors and those who preyed on them. Clint's growing reputation had him soon in the job of town marshal.

One day while stopping by the mayor's home, he saw one of the most beautiful women he had ever seen. Mayor Lucus introduced his daughter, Martha, to him. Clint tipped his hat and said, "Delighted to meet you, ma'am."

Martha caught her breath and blushed as she eyed this handsome and athletic young man with a marshal's badge. "Likewise, sir," she said as she curtseyed.

"Perhaps I'll see you at the barn dance tonight," said Clint.

Martha, who rarely went to those dances, responded, "I'll look forward to it."

Mayor Lucus, who worried about his daughter's solitude, was happy to see the exchange.

That evening a large crowd of townspeople gathered at a large barn in town. Clint arrived in his Sunday best and immediately spotted Martha standing by her father.

Gathering his courage, Clint walked over to Martha and asked her, "May I have the first dance?"

Martha smiled, blinked her eyes, and responded, "Why, certainly, sir."

The square dance caller began "do si do and face your sides." With that, groups of four gathered and the fiddler began.

Clint was charmed with the smooth flowing dance steps of Martha and the way her skirt flowed out, exposing her lovely legs, as he twirled her around.

After an hour of square dancing, the folks were given some line dancing music, and that was followed by waltzes. Martha remained Clint's partner the entire evening. Dancing with Martha to a waltz made Clint feel that he was floating on air. Was he falling in love again?

Martha clung to Clint, and felt her emotions overtake her. Clint was about the handsomest, most polite, and best dancer that she had ever met. When he held her, she felt safe and all warm inside. Could she be falling in love with this stranger?

In the days that followed, Clint found excuses to visit the mayor at his home, hoping for a glance of Martha. On the couple of times that he did, she gave him a beautiful smile. It was actually Martha who made the next step. On a sunny summer day Martha dropped by Clint's office to invite him to a picnic, consuming food that she had prepared.

When Clint arrived that afternoon, Martha was already saddled and holding a basket, which she handed to Clint to carry. Clint was extremely happy to be riding with Martha as he viewed the tree covered high mountain peaks surrounding them. They rode to a stream that joined others to form the headwaters of the Arkansas River. Martha spread out a blanket by the water. Rainbow trout could be spotted swimming in the stream.

Martha had prepared a dinner of fried chicken, potato salad, corn on the cob, green beans, and corn bread. They ate with gusto. Later they lay by the stream watching the trout swim by and making small talk, when Clint leaned over and gentled kissed Martha. Martha responded by holding on to Clint and kissing him back passionately. Clint, not trusting himself, said, "Martha, we had better head back."

From that day on they were together at every opportunity, until six months later, Clint sought the mayor out alone and asked if he could propose to Martha.

"Clint I have reservations about you marrying Martha. You are the perfect man for my Martha, a true gentleman, competent, caring, and kind, except for one thing: you are in a dangerous business, and could be gravely wounded or killed any day. That being said, I know she loves you, and I assent my son."

"Thank you, sir—and now I better find Martha!"

Martha was saddled and ready to go on a picnic. They went to their favorite spot near the stream. After dining Clint asked Martha to stand, then getting on one knee, he pulled a ring from his pocket, and looking into Martha's eyes said, "My darling, Martha, I have been to a great number of places, and I have done a great number of things, but never have I felt so much in love as I do now. Would you do me the honor of being my wife? I promise to always love you, and to care for you."

Martha blushed, held her hands to her cheeks, and responded, "Clint, my darling, I love you so much, and have from that day we first danced together, I will be your wife and love, honor and obey you forever!"

The wedding was set for June. They found a little cottage that they could rent in town. Then it happened. Martha and Clint were together in the marshal's office when a booming voice shouted, "Marshal, come on out and meet me face-to-face! You lying skunk. You murdered my brother!"

Clint got up and checked the ammunition load of his hand-gun and its proper seating in his holster. As he started for the door, Martha jumped up and put her arms around Clint, saying, "Don't go out there, Clint, please. Your deputy is due back any time now. Surely he can take care of it." When Clint continued walking toward the door, Martha jumped on his back and, with shrill anxiety, screamed, "No no, Clint, stop, I am begging you!"

Clint calmly removed her arms from his neck and said, "Martha, I must do this."

Martha continued to cry "No no no" and tried to grab Clint again, but lost her hold and fell to the floor. Clint opened the door and carefully peered out. The man doing the shouting was James Gannon, a.k.a. the Colorado Kid, a gunfighter who had nineteen notches in his belt.

"What's your beef, Gannon?"

"You bastard, you murdered my brother!"

"That's because he tried to draw on me like you're doing now! Back off and no one will get hurt today, and you can ride right of town. If you're going to draw do it now!"

From behind him, he heard Martha scream, "Don't do it, Clint!

At that moment, Gannon went for his gun.

Two shots reverberated through the town.

Gannon smiled and then fell to the ground. Clint's shot had gone through his heart and his spine, and was later found one-half mile beyond.

Clint holstered his weapon and turned to go back to his office, but was met by a very angry Martha. "You could have gotten yourself killed!" She was furious. "I think you like killing! I could never be a wife to you. Here take your ring back!"

Clint was stunned. His plans for living with a loving and caring wife for the rest of his life were completely shattered. What had he done to merit this treatment? It was his job after all. He loved Martha with his whole being.

Martha stormed back to her home and immediately went to bed without even saying hello to her father. Tears rolled down her face as she sobbed uncontrollably. She had ended a relationship with a man that she had loved very much, and with whom she wanted to live forever. She had made a big mistake!

Over the next several days, Clint immersed himself in his work. To keep himself busy he did double rounds. On one such round, the Allan gang came to town to rob the bank. Clint saw them arrive and leave their horses in front of the bank. There were six of them, all dirty and mean looking. Clint ran back to his office to get his shotgun and then stationed himself at the corner of the bank. Shots were fired, screams heard, and then the gang came running out of the bank. Clint let go with both barrels into the midst of the gang. Several robbers went down, but Clint received some return fire, and felt the impact of a bullet to his upper leg. He fell while drawing his six-gun. Clint fired on the bandits still standing before passing out. When he awoke, he was in bed with Doc Stevens tending to him. "You are a very lucky man, marshal, the bullet nicked your femoral artery and you lost a lot of blood. A passerby saw you bleeding out and put a tourniquet on your leg. Years ago I would have amputated the leg, but I have since learned how to repair blood vessels, so you will keep your leg, sir."

Clint thanked the doctor and then asked where he was. "You are in a bedroom of the mayor's house. He insisted that you recover here. You'll be in bed for weeks while your leg heals. Any attempt to walk or stress the leg before it heals could open your wound and you would bleed to death. After the doctor left, Martha entered the room. "Clint, you are a hero. The whole town is alive in praise for you. Just about everybody kept their money in that bank. I will care for you now and forever if you will take me back. I am so sorry for the things I said. I found my ring in your pocket. May I have it back?"

Clint, his heart beating for joy, responded, "Of course, my darling, you may have now and forever!"

Clint had finally stopped wandering. The Walkers had four children. A great-great-grandson moved from Colorado to Wisconsin and became the governor of that state.

ABOUT THE AUTHOR

Rod Sorkin is retired and lives in Carmel, Indiana, in the Indianapolis metropolitan area. He was born and raised in New York City and attended the Cooper Union School of Engineering, where he received the bachelor of electronic engineering and was awarded the Goodman Humanities Prize. He later received the master of science degree in electronic engineering from Ohio State University. He also completed the Harvard University Kennedy School of Government Program for senior executives and the Johns Hopkins/Syracuse University National Security Senior Leadership Course. Before retiring, he worked in intelligence for the US Department of Defense for thirty-two years, living in Maryland near the Chesapeake Bay. Rod was awarded the National Intelligence Distinguished Service Medal and Presidential Rank Award of Distinguished Executive in public service. *The Wandering Cowboy* is his second fictional work. He is the author of the novel *Redemption* (Page Publishing 2015) and the technical book *Integrated Electronics* (McGraw-Hill 1970). Rod was inspired to write *The Wandering Cowboy* by his love for classic westerns from the likes of Zane Gray, Max Brand, Louis L'Amour, and William Johnstone, among others. Although living with some physical disability from a stroke, Rod enjoys time spent with his two grandsons, and he has taken to writing as a creative outlet. He has also edits and publishes a monthly literary journal for his retirement community.

CPSIA information can be obtained
at www.ICGtesting.com
Printed in the USA
FFOW04n0218200916
27741FF